W/D SALE

WHEELS ROLL WEST

WHEELS ROLL WEST

by

Wayne D. Overholser

The Golden West Large Print Books
Long Preston, North Yorkshire,
BD23 4ND, England.

British Library Cataloguing in Publication Data.

Overholser, Wayne D.
Wheels roll west.

A catalogue record of this book is
available from the British Library

ISBN 978-1-84262-937-6 pbk

Published in Large Print 2013 by arrangement with
Golden West Literary Agency

The Golden West Large Print is an imprint of Library Magna
Books Ltd.

Printed and bound in Great Britain by
T.J. (International) Ltd., Cornwall, PL28 8RW

Chapter One

By three in the afternoon Jim Horn had located a suitable camp ground along the Arkansas River, just below where Lost Creek came tumbling in from the south. He turned back downriver, riding slowly, for there was no hurry now. Tomorrow the Ohio to Colorado colony would make the last day's journey up the creek to Lost Valley and Horn's job would be finished. Angus Morgan would pay him off tonight, probably without even a thank you, and he'd ride on just as he had been riding on for most of his twenty-eight years.

Well, it was all right. There were plenty of opportunities in Colorado for a man if he wanted to look for them. But maybe he didn't. Maybe he was the proverbial rolling stone that never gathered any moss. It had always been fun to keep rolling, and there was a lot of country he hadn't seen. But now he'd met Ruth Morgan.

He rounded a turn in the river and saw her riding toward him, tall and straight in the saddle, the most graceful woman he had ever seen. He reined up to wait for her, wondering how she had managed to get away from her father's wagon that she had been driving. He wondered, too, why his heart began to pound.

Foolish! Just plain damned foolish! Like a kid falling in love for the first time. He was too old to act like this. He'd traveled alone too long to lose his head over a woman. But Ruth Morgan was a very special woman, good-looking and strong and filled with a great vitality. Much of the time she seemed as cool and distant as a glittering star in a black sky.

She rode up to him, smiling, and asked: 'Find a good place?'

He held his answer for a moment, his eyes fixed on her. Her hat dangled down her back from a chin strap, and her black hair, carefully pinned up that morning, was now wind-ruffled and loose. Her brown eyes met his, and he sensed the restlessness that was in her, the discontent of a woman who was still sampling life and had not yet found what she wanted.

Nodding, he jerked a thumb upstream. 'About a quarter of a mile from here.'

'Shade?'

He nodded again. 'Some big cottonwoods.'

'Let's have a look,' she said, and swung upriver.

He reined his black gelding in beside the girl, glancing sideways at her. Viewed from the side, her chin was a little defiant. Looking at her this way, he was unable to see the dimple that he knew was there. Jim thought back to the spring day in Fort Wallace when Ruth's father, Angus Morgan, had asked him to guide the colony to Lost Valley and decided he'd been a chuckle-headed idiot for saying yes. Sure, he'd been out of a job at the time, but being out of a job had never worried him. Looking at it now with cool objectivity, he knew he would not have taken the job if he had not met Ruth Morgan and known that she would be going with the colony.

She glanced at him, frowning. 'What's the matter, my face dirty?'

'No. I'm just taking a good look. Sort of wanted to put a picture of it in my mind.'

The frown faded out. 'Why?'

'In an hour or so your dad will pay me off. Don't reckon I'll be seeing you any more, and I wanted to remember what you looked like.'

She gave him a pleased smile. 'I'm surprised, Jim. I didn't think you were interested in anything but camping places and water holes and grass for the stock and such.'

She was looking straight ahead again, her chin tilted more defiantly than usual. No, it wouldn't do. He'd best forget her. She wasn't the kind who would ride over the nearest hill just to see what was there. She'd find a spot along the river she liked and she'd stay: *Let's build a cabin here and you plow the ground and raise a crop. After a while other folks will come and you'll be rich and respectable, and I'll go to church and be president of the Ladies' Aid.* Well, that wasn't for Jim Horn. Not by a jug full!

'I always figured a man was a fool to reach for what he couldn't have,' he said.

'How do you know you can't have it?' she demanded. 'If you think I'm engaged to Rusty Hancock...' She stopped as if not quite sure whether she was or not.

Horn said, 'Rusty figures you are. I'll bet he's driving your wagon right now so you could take a ride.'

'Well, suppose he is?' The chin was definitely defiant. 'I never told Rusty I'd marry him. Besides, he's just a kid.'

He was that, all right, Horn thought. Not yet twenty-one, Rusty Hancock had the look of a potato sprout that had grown too fast – a lot of bone but not much meat. Ruth wasn't any older, but she had matured. She had the right curves in the right places, balanced up as pretty as if the Lord had given her His special attention, and Horn had a feeling that she possessed all the desires and passions that a man wanted his woman to have.

'Rusty might be worth waiting for,' Horn said. 'Your pa kind o' favors him.'

'It's just that his folks were Dad's friends,' she said quickly, 'and he has Rusty's money to invest. I ... I...' She bit her lip. 'I shouldn't have said that. Nobody knows about it but Dad and Rusty and me.'

'And Webb.'

'Oh, no. Dad wouldn't talk ... wouldn't tell him.'

'Gold enough to build a big, purty place up yonder in Lost Valley.' Horn shook his head. 'Crazy dreaming. Your whole outfit is like a bunch of children. Why in thunder didn't they stay in Ohio?'

'Because there's opportunity in Colorado,' she flung at him. 'Because people working together can perform miracles.' She stopped and looked at him accusingly. 'You don't believe any of those things, do you?'

'No. I mean, yes, but there's one thing the

West taught me a long time ago. A man who's worth a damn stands on his two legs, and he doesn't depend on his neighbors giving him a third one.'

'You mean Dad. I know you don't think we'll make a go of it. Right from the day we left Fort Wallace you told Dad we wouldn't.'

He shrugged. 'That's just my notion. Angus Morgan's is something else. Looks like he's got the ideas and Rusty's putting up the *dinero*.'

The defiance had gone out of her. She said somberly: 'That's about it. Stay with us, Jim. We're going to need you.'

They had reached the camping place, and Horn reined up. 'This is it,' he said.

Ruth looked at the grassy bench above the Arkansas, at the giant cottonwoods and the cool patch of shade surrounded by dazzling sunlight, and then she glanced at the river, running high and cold now in late spring. 'It's a pretty place,' she murmured, and swung out of the saddle.

He stepped down, leaving the reins dangling. He stood close to her, a full head taller, his hair, as light as new rope, falling to his shoulders. He rubbed his hands along his dirty buckskins, thinking that this was the first time in all the weeks they had spent at Fort Wallace getting ready and in the passage across the wind-chilled Kansas and Colorado plains that Ruth had shown any real interest in him. Now she turned, her face lifted to his.

'I'm afraid, Jim.' She put a hand on his arm. 'I don't know why, but I'm afraid.'

'You ought to be. Trouble is your dad knows so much he doesn't need any advice.'

She stepped away from him, her eyes turning upstream. 'I know. He's just too smart for his good or anyone else's. He's always been that way.'

It was the first time he had heard her say that she understood Angus Morgan's weakness, for a weakness it was. He had gathered the colonists from the farms and small towns of southern Ohio, painting a rosy picture of their future in Colorado. He had sent Ike Webb, a one-man locating committee, to select their future homes, and Webb had picked Lost Valley. It was a poor choice, but when Horn had tried to tell Morgan that before they had left Fort Wallace, the colony leader had blown up.

'Webb has seen the valley,' Morgan had shouted, 'and I trust Ike Webb's judgment when it comes to land! Your job is to get us there. That's all. Just get us there.'

Horn had not mentioned it again. It was their money they were spending, their time and their labor, and the broken dreams would be theirs, too. If they had enough money to live through the first hard years, they might in time learn how to farm the high valley with its hard winters and short summers. Horn had never inquired about the colonists' financial backlog, but he was reasonably certain from talk he'd heard that they expected to raise a crop this year. If they didn't, they'd starve the following winter. And there was Newt Kimmel who would not stand for a bunch of greenhorns swarming all over his Clawhammer range.

There was nothing right about this thing. Angus Morgan was honest enough, but he was a pig-headed fool. If young Rusty Hancock wanted to throw his money away at Morgan's say-so, that was Rusty's business. He was young and strong, and he could start again, but it was different with the rest of them. Middle-aged men with families, farmers and craftsmen of one kind or another, they had taken Morgan's word, and they'd lose their shirts. The shirts might not be much, but when they were all people had, it was a hell of a bad thing.

Horn pulled Ruth around to face him. He said: 'This isn't any of my business, which same your dad is going to tell me, but I hate to go off and leave a band of sheep in the same pasture with a pack of wolves.'

'What are you getting at, Jim?'

'These people are licked before they get to Lost Valley. Maybe your dad would listen to you. Get 'em to go north where a farmer can raise something.'

She stood very close to him, her face grave.

'Jim, Jim, I'm just a woman. Men never listen to women.'

'You're a mighty pretty one,' he said, 'and men listen to pretty women.'

'Then why don't you listen to me? Stay with us, Jim. The wolves won't bother the sheep if you're around.'

There was nothing cold or distant about her now. Her lips, red and full, were parted, the smile lingering at their corners. Impulsively he pulled her to him and kissed her, holding her hard against his body, kissed her thoroughly and passionately. Her arms came up around his neck, and she clung to him, and, when he let her go, she still clung to him, her head against his chest.

'Jim, you were such a long time getting around to that,' she whispered. 'It isn't up to the woman to do the chasing, you know. That's a man's job.'

He stared down at her, fighting a sudden rush of panic. The next thing he knew he'd be married, and she'd be wanting him to stay with the colony, she'd want him tied up to something that had been bound to fail from the beginning.

'I wasn't thinking about chasing or anything,' he said lamely. 'I mean, I'm not one to settle down, and you aren't the kind who'd follow me all over the country.'

She stepped back, her face red. 'All right, Mister Horn, so you aren't the kind to settle down. Well, a kiss doesn't mean anything to me, either.'

'It isn't that,' he said quickly. 'It's just that I'm not sticking with this here colony, and you wouldn't go with me.'

Horn had not heard Angus Morgan and Ike Webb ride up, and he was not aware of their presence until Morgan's big voice boomed out: 'I've got one question to ask you, Horn. What are your intentions regarding my daughter?'

Horn wheeled, red-faced. 'Right now I don't have any intentions.'

Morgan stepped down from the saddle. He was a big man, tall, broad of shoulder, impressive-appearing with his dark, piercing eyes and heavy black beard. He had the look and bearing of a leader, but actually his talent for leadership had never been put to the test. Now, meeting the big man's eyes, Horn wondered how much of Morgan's swagger was skin-deep.

'I saw you kissing her,' Morgan boomed. 'Rusty Hancock considers himself engaged to her, and I favor Rusty. I know him. I don't know you. Sometimes I think you're half savage.'

'And I ought to go live with the Utes.' Horn motioned to the narrow cañon through which Lost Creek tumbled northward to meet the Arkansas. 'There's your route to Lost Valley. Give me my two hundred dollars and I'll be riding.'

Ruth had been listening, saying nothing. Now she walked toward her father, her head held high. 'I made him kiss me,' she said, 'because I favor him. We need him, all of us.'

'We don't need him,' Ike Webb said in his blustering voice 'We're only one day's journey from the valley. Pay him off, Angus.'

19

'Sure,' Horn said softly. 'Let Webb take you up the cañon.'

'Don't think I can't!' Webb cried. 'We didn't need you in the first place, and we don't need you now. Ruth's just silly about your damned long hair.'

Horn liked almost everyone in the colony. He respected people who had no illusions about themselves and who were willing to take a gamble to better their conditions, but he disliked Morgan because of his conceit, and he distrusted Ike Webb. Webb was a short, squat man with a shrewd, animal-like cunning in his green eyes that made Horn wary of him. Actually he had no grounds for his suspicions beyond the fact that Webb had picked Lost Valley.

'I'm kind of curious about you, Webb,' Horn said.

'What do you mean by that?' Webb demanded.

'I think you're a crook,' Horn answered.

Webb swore, and his right hand dug for his gun, but at that moment his horse began to pitch, and Webb, caught by surprise with his gun half drawn, was thrown to the ground. He sat up, spluttering, his dignity injured more than his body, and found himself looking into Horn's .45.

'You're a fool, Webb,' Horn said evenly. 'You try that with someone else and they'll be digging a hole to plant you in.'

'All right, all right now!' Morgan shouted. 'Put your guns up. No need of trouble. You were out of line, Horn, and I'll hear no more of it. I've told you many times that I trust Webb implicitly.'

'And that makes you the fool,' Horn said hotly. 'Give me my pay and I'll get the hell out of here.'

'No.' Ruth slipped her arm through Horn's as if to hold him against his will, defiant eyes on her father. 'Jim knows this country, Dad. Listen to him.'

'I'll listen to nobody. I'm the president of this colony.' Morgan stroked his beard, gaze swinging to Ruth and back to Horn. Then he said grudgingly: 'All right, Horn. Stay with us till we reach the valley.'

'The hell I will. The agreement we made was for me to fetch you to the mouth of Lost Creek. You're here.'

'I'll give you fifty dollars to stay with us till we reach the valley,' Morgan said heavily.

Ruth's arm tightened against Horn's. She whispered: 'Please, Jim. One more day. For me.'

Horn hesitated, and then against his better judgment he said: 'All right, one more day.' He would not have done this for anyone but Ruth.

He walked toward his horse, deeply troubled. He had always been contemptuous of a man who surrendered his independence of mind to a woman. Now he had done exactly that.

The wagons came rolling around the point, young Rusty Hancock in the lead driving the Morgan wagon. Horn staked out his horse close to the base of the hill and, walking back to the river, watched the wagons come, swaying canvas tops dirty and weather-stained, horses sweat-gummed and thinned down by the countless miles they had traveled.

Horn hunkered at the river's edge, rolled a smoke, and fired it as he thought idly of his drifting years. He'd served with the Colorado volunteers at the battle of Glorietta Pass when the West had been saved for the Union. He'd done a number of things since – hunted buffalo for a railroad, ridden for Newt Kimmel's Clawhammer in Lost Valley, and carried a star in one of the Colorado mining camps. He'd even had a shot at mining.

Jack-of-all-trades, Horn thought bitterly, a drifter who placed his own freedom of movement and spirit above everything else. In a way he envied the stolid men with small ambitions, men content to settle down and fight the elements in the hope of eventually owning their homes, men who married and raised a flock of dirty-faced kids and were satisfied to sleep with their wives in one-room shacks and eat salt side and beans.

There were the others, the ambitious ones like Angus Morgan who dreamed king-size dreams. There were the Ike Webbs who flattered the ambitious ones, shrewd, scheming men who usually came out ahead in the end, their pockets filled with the gold of the men they flattered. It took all kinds to make the world, Horn thought as he watched the colonists make camp for the night. There was the usual clatter and rustle, the running and calling from one wagon to another, the laughter and shouts of children as they raced along the riverbank. Wood smoke rose from a dozen cook fires. There was the smell of it and the smell of coffee and frying bacon that made a man remember his belly was empty.

People like these colonists had settled the West. There had been the go-backs who had failed during the hard days following the first gold rush to Colorado, there had been the others who had stayed and bucked it through. Many of them had done well. It all depended on what was in a man, and Horn wondered about these people. Were they the go-backs of a later generation, or did they have what it took to hang and rattle? He didn't know. Only the pressure of time and privation would tell.

The restlessness grew in Horn until his nerves were trigger tight. He watched Ruth working at her cook fire, saw Morgan talking to Ike Webb who was flaring back and pounding a fist against the palm of his hand. He saw lank Rusty Hancock care for Morgan's horses and then come stalking toward him. From the look on the boy's bony face, Jim knew this could be trouble.

Rusty came up and hunkered beside him. He said: 'I want to talk to you, Horn.' The boy rolled a cigarette, his hands trembling a little. 'I know you can kill me and I sure as hell ain't no ring-tailed wowser when it comes to guns or knives, but just the same I'm fixing to tell you what you are.'

Horn studied the boy's taut face. The sun was down now, and the cool of early evening was settling upon the cañon bottom. Rusty took off his hat and laid it beside him, reddish hair tousled. He was tall and ungainly from growing too fast; his long nose and long chin gave his face a sharp-featured look. The makings of a man were in him. Given time, he'd do, but now he was a little wild with the brashness of youth, and Horn considered it a bad gamble to bet on his reaching old age.

'Go ahead,' Horn repeated. 'I always wondered what I was.'

Rusty fired his cigarette, staring at Horn through the smoke with grim belligerence. He said: 'Angus said he caught you kissing Ruth.'

'I kissed her,' Horn said, 'but there wasn't no getting caught about it.'

'She's spoken for,' Rusty said. 'We growed up together in Ohio. My family lived next to the Morgans. I've loved her as long as I can remember. Now you come along, a damned half Indian, and you kiss her.'

'Take it easy, kid. Ruth doesn't tell it that way.'

'She did till you came along.' Rusty threw his cigarette into the river. 'You're different than anything she ever seen before. She'd have been satisfied to settle down with me in Lost Valley, but now she'll think of you as long as she lives. I ain't good enough for her now.'

'A man doesn't deserve a woman he can't win,' Horn said. 'I don't reckon either you or me will tell her who to marry. She'll make up her own mind.'

Rusty was silent a moment, a hand rubbing his chin. Then he said: 'Well, she's got it made up. I can tell you that. And I'm telling you something else, mister. You'd better treat her right. Settle down and give her a home, or I'll... I'll...' he stopped and took a long breath, then he asked: 'Well, what are you going to do?'

'I don't know,' Horn said. 'I aimed to ride out of camp tonight but Morgan asked me to stay another day till you got to the valley.'

'You love her, don't you?' Rusty demanded.

Horn hesitated, knowing that loving her

and marrying her were two different things. He said finally: 'Yes, but I'm not sure I'll ask her to marry me. Like it's been said, I reckon I'm half Indian.'

Rusty's hands fisted. 'But you'll marry her just the same, and you'll take her away with you. You'll take her to hell-an'-gone, and she won't have nothing.'

'What do you aim to do?'

Rusty kept rubbing his chin, staring at the river. 'I don't know, but if I married her, I'd give her a home and I'd do all I could to make her happy.'

'I want her to be happy,' Horn said, 'but there's one thing you haven't figured on. Suppose you lost your money?'

Rusty pinned searching eyes on Horn's face. 'Why would I lose my money?'

'You've given it to Morgan, haven't you?'

'How did you know?'

'Ruth told me.'

'She shouldn't have said...' Rusty stopped. He picked up a rock, and threw it into the river. 'Yeah, and I've been scared ever since we left home. Angus was what I'd call a failure in Ohio, but he's a good talker. When he's talking, you forget the things he ain't done. You just think about the things he says he's gonna do. Besides, I thought it was one way to make Ruth love me.'

Ruth turned from the cook fire, calling: 'Supper!'

'All right.' Horn rose. 'Rusty, we both love Ruth. If you're the one who can make her happy, I won't get in your way.'

The boy got to his feet. Some of the antagonism had gone out of his face. 'I can say the same to you.' He cleared his throat. 'Ruth says we need you. Not just for tomorrow but for a long time. You know the country, and I don't trust Ike Webb no farther than I can throw my horse by the tail. Will you stay with us?'

Horn ran his boot toe through the gravel, staring down at the mark. This was the last thing he had expected from Rusty. He could curse the day he had signed on with the colony, but that wouldn't do any good. If he rode off, he would never forget he had left these people. They'd lose out and some would die, and it would be on his conscience.

Ruth had turned again from the fire. Seeing that they hadn't started toward the wagon, she called again, sharply this time: 'Supper!'

'Coming!' Horn shouted.

He raised his eyes to Rusty's face. He saw the fear and the worry that were there. Rusty Hancock stood to lose both his money and his girl. It was enough to make any man worry.

'I ain't one to beg,' Rusty said doggedly, 'but I'm begging now. For Ruth and me and all of us.'

'I'd stay,' Horn said at last, 'if I knew I could help, but Morgan won't listen to me.'

'We'll make him listen,' Rusty said grimly. 'There's more talk about him than you know. Were all worried.'

'I'll think it over,' Horn said, and swung toward the Morgan wagon.

When they came up, Ruth said with some

asperity: 'It took you a long time to get here.'

'Big palaver,' Horn said.

Webb usually ate with the Morgans, but he was not around tonight. Angus Morgan hunkered by a wagon wheel, eating with wolfish relish, ignoring Horn's presence. Night had settled down around them, the last color fading from the western horizon, and on both sides of them the ridges were lost to sight, merged into the blackness of the sky.

There was silence all around them, the weird, haunting silence of the wilderness. It was a thing to frighten people who were not used to it. Horn understood how it was with the colonists. They had come from a settled land, had rolled across empty plains where they could see for miles in any direction. The Rockies had slowly taken form before them, Pike's Peak raising its great, barren shoulders to the sky.

Now they were deep in the Shining Mountains, and the cañon walls pressed against them. Tomorrow they would see the valley that had been promised to them. Tonight the worries and fears that had been growing in them had suddenly become monstrous. Lost Valley might turn out to be a worthless desert or it might be the Promised Land that Angus Morgan had talked about in such glowing terms. They weren't sure, and so much depended on it.

Horn put down his empty coffee cup. 'Where's the fiddler, Ruth?'

She had been leaning over the cook fire. Now she turned to him, her face flushed by the heat. 'A couple of wagons from here. Why?'

'He'd better tune up. This camp feels like a funeral being born.'

She shook her head. 'He won't play, Jim. I asked him a while ago.'

Morgan rose. His voice lacked its usual booming quality of certainty when he said: 'Something's wrong. Ought to be dancing and singing, one day away from the end of the trip, but they're sitting around like it was a wake.'

'We'll stir 'em up, some way,' Horn said.

He would have said more if he had not heard horses coming down Lost Creek. He rose, putting his tin plate and cup on the ground. He had expected this, but they were later than he had thought they would be. Morgan heard them then, and stood rigidly, his head cocked, listening.

Someone farther down the river yelled: 'Indians!'

Another man bawled: 'Get your rifles or we'll lose our hair!'

'No Indians around here, are there, Horn?' Morgan demanded.

'We wouldn't hear them if there were.' Horn ran toward the men who had shouted, calling: 'Leave your rifles in the wagons. These men aren't Indians.'

He heard women cry out in relief, heard men curse in low voices, and one demanded: 'Then who in hell would be riding in at night like this?'

'We'll find out. Come up to Morgan's wagon. If there is trouble, I'll handle it.'

Horn swung around. 'Rusty, throw some wood on the fire.'

Horn walked back, more worried than he would admit. He knew what panic could do. If the colonists got boogery and someone fired a shot, there would be hell to pay. Even as he strode toward the wagon, he heard a woman cry: 'What are we doing in this God-forsaken country, Carl? Just try to tell me.'

It was the Larsons. Carl Larson was one of the trustees of the colony, a carpenter by trade, but little different from the farmers and the rest, just a man with a family who had believed Angus Morgan. His voice came to Horn, quite calm: 'God never forsakes a country where His people are. Let's remember that, Sadie.'

His words stilled the worry that had risen in Horn. The little people were like that. Give them half a chance and they'd make out. They'd be afraid, they'd fuss and fume and wish they were back home, but when the chips were down, they'd come through if they had the right leadership. That was the trouble. Angus Morgan was not the right leader.

Horn came to Morgan's fire that had flamed up and was throwing a flickering light on Ruth and Rusty who stood between it and the wagon. Morgan had crawled into his wagon. When he came out, he carried a Winchester.

Horn said: 'Put it back, Morgan.'

Morgan squared his big shoulders, and his head jutted forward. 'Don't give me orders, Horn. 'I'm thinking we made a mistake asking you to stay.'

'That may be,' Horn said, 'but it was a bigger mistake when they elected you president of this colony.'

'Do what he says, Dad,' Ruth urged.

Rusty picked up the axe. 'Put it back, Angus. Let's see how Horn handles this.'

Morgan held the rifle on the ready, fighting his pride, black eyes alive with the desire to kill the man who defied him. Horn met his gaze, right hand wrapped around gun butt. He said: 'Morgan, you're like a good-looking horse that you ride hard for fifty yards and then he caves. Put that Winchester back.'

He broke as Horn had been sure he would. No bottom to him, no real talent for leadership. He had been a failure in Ohio, Rusty Hancock had said, and he'd be a failure here. Some men were like that, hoping a change of scenery would make heroes out of them, but it never did.

Morgan made a slow turn and slid the rifle into the wagon. Then he faced Horn, saying sullenly: 'You'd better know what you're doing.'

Horn said nothing. He eased his gun into leather and moved to stand by the fire, aware of the crowd that had gathered behind him. The incoming horses were still hidden by the darkness. Five or six of them, Horn judged

He asked: 'Where's Webb, Ruth?'

'I don't know,' she answered. 'I haven't seen him for an hour or more.'

The riders came to the edge of the firelight,

and one called out: 'What outfit is this?'

Horn had expected to see Newt Kimmel and some of his Clawhammer crew, but these men were strangers to him. He answered: 'The Ohio-Colorado colony.'

'Where you headed?'

'Lost Valley.'

The speaker swung out of the saddle, the rest remaining where they were. A tough lot, Horn saw, all but their leader packing guns on their hips and Winchesters in their scabbards. The one who had spoken reared back, hands in his pockets. He seemed different from the others – a dude, perhaps a gambler from Pueblo. He was wearing a ruffled silk shirt and a dove-colored broadcloth suit. Now he lifted his white Stetson and bowed to Ruth. His chestnut brown hair was slicked down, and, when he spoke, his voice was velvet smooth.

'You're a fair woman to find in such a wild country. You belong in Denver, not out here where your beautiful black hair will eventually adorn some Ute teepee.'

Horn heard the girl catch her breath. He said hotly: 'State your business, friend.'

The dude brought his gaze to Horn. 'A long hair, by the eternal. Do I have the pleasure of speaking with Wild Bill Hickok?'

'I'm Jim Horn. I guided this outfit from Fort Wallace.'

'Why don't you cut your hair?'

'Why are you wearing them dude britches?'

The man laughed with his mouth but not with his eyes. He motioned to the others who stepped out of their saddles, one of them moving aside to stand by himself. A gunslinger, Horn saw, with two black-butted .44s carried low and thonged down. He was a slender, pale-eyed man, typical of those who made killing their business. The plan was plain to read. They had brought this man along to kill anyone who gave them trouble.

'Why, that's fair enough,' the dude said, his voice still soft. 'I'm Clay Vance, representing the Rocky Mountain Land Company. Who's the leader of this party?'

Morgan stepped forward, glowing with the

importance of his position. He said: 'I am. What can I do for you?'

Something was wrong here, terribly wrong, but at the moment Horn could not put his finger on it. Ike Webb was not in camp. Perhaps Morgan had told him about Rusty Hancock's money. That might be it. Or it might be something else. Horn had never heard of Clay Vance or the Rocky Mountain Land Company. If the company was big and legitimate, he would have heard of it.

Vance was silent for a moment, eyes sweeping the crowd and wagons. Then he stepped forward, right hand extended. 'I'm pleased to meet you, Mister...?'

'Morgan. Angus Morgan.' He took Vance's hand, his sense of importance growing. 'We left Ohio last fall with more than two hundred souls ... men, women, and children. Everyone is a worker, Mister Vance. A few of the men are single, but most of them are family men. All of us have one thing in common. We expect to make our homes here and to grow with Colorado. We are a co-operative colony, working together for the common good.'

'A commendable undertaking, sir.' Vance's eyes touched Ruth's face. 'This is your daughter, I presume. I seem to see a resemblance.'

'That's right,' Morgan said indulgently. 'I'm proud of her, and, as you can see, I have a right to be.'

'What's your business, Vance?' Horn cut in.

Morgan wheeled on Horn, outraged. 'Keep in your place, Horn. Whatever business our visitors have is with me.'

'I said I'd handle the trouble,' Horn said, 'and that I aim to do.'

'There is no trouble,' Morgan said.

Horn gave him a thin grin. 'You know, Morgan, a man can smell trouble if he has a nose for it, but you couldn't smell a skunk if he fired under your nose.'

'You can't smell what isn't here, my friend,' Vance said smoothly. 'Now, Mister Morgan, I presume you have some capital.'

Morgan nodded, swinging back to Vance.

'Enough to get a start. We hope to be in Lost Valley tomorrow night. We will begin at once to clear the land and get in a crop. For a time we will live in tents. Houses can wait till fall, but crops cannot.'

'Quite right, quite right. Now one more question. You have artisans as well as farmers, I suppose?'

'Certainly. As a matter of fact, we have brought a small sawmill with us that will be set up at once. We plan to erect a colony building that will house a store, an office, and a school room. We will not neglect the education of our children. We have a teacher with us, several carpenters, blacksmiths, and tinsmiths. We'll also have a gristmill. You can see that we have no consumptives among us, no weaklings. Every member of our colony was carefully selected from the best people in Ohio.'

'You've done a fine job, Mister Morgan,' Vance said. 'Your people are the kind we need in Colorado. As you doubtless know, statehood is not far ahead for us.' He coughed apologetically. 'But I am forced to give you bad news. You will not settle in Lost Valley.'

Morgan's face went blank. Ruth cried out involuntarily, and someone in the crowd began to curse. It was Rusty Hancock who moved into the firelight, demanding: 'What do you mean by that?'

Vance swung to one of the men behind him. 'I'd like for you folks to meet Ben Travis. Tell them, Ben.'

Travis, a burly man with a ragged beard, stepped up beside Vance. He took off his hat, raised a hand to his round head, and scratched it. 'It's purty damned lucky for you folks that Clay Vance happened to be here, or we'd have come a-shooting. I represent the settlers of Lost Valley. There ain't no room for you. I'm right sorry, but that's the truth of it.'

'Now hold on,' Morgan fumed. 'We sent a man to Colorado last summer before we left Ohio. He spent some time in Lost Valley looking it over, and he told us there were no settlers in the valley.'

Travis laughed shortly. 'We're there just the same, and we don't aim to let no green-horns come in and push us out.'

'But ... but ... there must be room for us,' Morgan whispered.

'Room?' Travis laughed again. 'Sure, if you want to go to the south end of the valley that's as dry as a bone. If that's what you want, come ahead, but you'll starve in a year. It'd take a goat to live down there.'

There was silence for a moment, the kind of silence that comes when people are too stunned to speak. Horn did not look at them. He knew what he would see on their faces; he knew how they felt. He still did not understand the game these men were playing, but it would come out now.

Morgan wheeled to face Horn. 'Why didn't you tell us about this?'

'You had faith in Webb,' Horn murmured. 'Remember?'

'Yeah,' Rusty said harshly. 'That's right, Angus. Horn tried to tell you, but you knew it all.'

'It's been several years since I was in the valley,' Horn said. 'At that time there were no settlers there. Just a ranch, Newt Kimmnel's Clawhammer. I figured, you might have trouble with him, but I didn't know about these yahoos.'

'If you was there a year ago,' Travis said in an ugly voice, 'you'd know...'

'I said *several* years ago,' Horn cut in.

'All right, several years. Anyhow, you'd have seen us. You've been worked, Morgan, and it's my guess the long hair done it.'

'I should have known!' Morgan shouted wildly. 'He worked us for a fee. That's all, a guide fee, but he hasn't been paid, and he won't be.'

'Dad, you're not being fair,' Ruth cried. 'If we've been deceived, it was Webb who did it.'

'I said I had faith in Webb!' Morgan shouted in a great voice. 'I still do.'

'I guess you've gabbled enough.' Horn nodded at Vance. 'I suppose you're a farmer, too. You look like one.'

Vance shook his head, smiling affably. 'You're wrong, long hair. I happened to be in Pueblo when I heard about you folks. I came on ahead to stop trouble. Otherwise, as Travis told you, they would have come shooting to protect their homes.'

'We'll still do some shooting,' Travis said truculently, 'if you greenhorns think you're gonna settle in Lost Valley.'

'These are reasonable people, Ben,' Vance said quickly. 'There need be no trouble. The instant I shook hands with Mister Morgan, I saw that he was both reasonable and intelligent. Now I have an alternative to offer, folks. My company owns a large grant of land some distance to the south. We'll be glad to have you settle there. That's why I asked the questions I did. I had to ascertain what sort of folks you were. You'll do, Mister Morgan.'

'Where's your grant?' Horn demanded.

'I'm talking to...'

'Where is it?' Horn asked again.

Vance licked his lips, his gaze flickering

toward the gunman as if to be sure he was still there. Then he said: 'It's on the Picketwire. You'll have to backtrack, and swing south, Mister Morgan, but it will pay you. How much land do you expect to take?'

'Twenty thousand acres.'

Vance nodded. 'I see. Well, we have several choice blocks you may choose from, Mister Morgan. It's good land. Plenty of water. Fine timber. And there is one thing you may not have thought about. We'll sell the land to you and you will have titles at once. If you were to settle in Lost Valley, you would have to preëmpt or homestead because it is government land.'

'Get on your horses and drift,' Horn said.

'Now wait...,' Morgan began.

'Stay out of it, Angus,' Rusty said in a hoarse voice. 'This looks like a cheating shenanigan to me. Before we make any deals, I want a look at Lost Valley.'

'Then you'll be looking at some hot lead,' Travis bawled.

Vance gave Rusty a pitying look. 'You're a

boy, my friend. Just a boy. The value of age is that wisdom comes with it. I judge your people are willing to follow Mister Morgan's advice, or they would not have chosen him for their leader.'

'Maybe we made a mistake.' It was Carl Larson, standing well back in the crowd. 'What's your idea on this, Horn?'

'I've got just one idea,' Horn said. 'Looks to me like Webb threw in with these yahoos to cheat you. Vance is lying as fast as a dog trots. I never heard of the Rocky Mountain Land Company, and I don't think there is any such outfit.'

The gunman moved forward, right hand hovering over gun butt. 'I'm a settler, long hair, and I don't cotton to being called any of the names you're giving us.'

Horn's eyes swung quickly to Vance and Travis and the rest. He saw anticipation in their eyes, sensed the cool certainty that was in them. The gunman, whoever he was, had been hired as insurance against just such a situation as Vance was facing now. They must have known that Jim Horn was with the colony, and that brought Horn's thinking to Ike Webb.

'You're no settler, mister,' Horn said evenly. 'Get back under the rock you just crawled out...'

The gunman made his draw, the fast sure movement of a man who lived by the gun, but still he was too slow to do the job. He had made the mistake of underestimating Jim Horn. Horn had his gun clear of leather before the other's Colt was leveled. He fired, the roar of the explosion rolling out into the quiet. The gunman's shot came like a belated echo, the slug kicking up dirt ten feet in front of him. He bent forward, a hand coming up, then he broke at knee and hip and spilled forward.

Horn swung his gun to cover Vance and his friends. He saw the shocked surprise that gripped them and heard Vance say: 'You *are* Hickok.'

'Pick him up.' Horn motioned to the dead man. 'Put him on a horse and git, the whole damned bunch of you.'

They obeyed in sullen silence, and, when they had mounted, Vance put his hands on his saddle horn and leaned forward, eyes filled with wickedness. 'I will tell you whoever tries to bring a wagon up Lost Creek will be shot.' Then, with Vance leading, they rode away into the darkness.

For a long moment there was no talk from the colonists, no movement. Then Morgan said in a shocked voice: 'You killed him.'

'I reckon I did.' Horn ejected the empty shell, and thumbed a new one into the cylinder. 'You know what would have happened if I hadn't?'

'He'd have killed you,' Rusty Hancock said.

Turning, Horn brought his gaze to Ruth's face. She stood as if paralyzed, her cheeks very pale. He thought bitterly: *Now* she *thinks I'm half Indian.*

'It was murder!' Morgan shouted, suddenly filled with righteous indignation. 'We have a position in our constitution and bylaws to take care of...'

Horn wheeled on him. 'You are a green-horn, Morgan, the greenest one I've ever seen. Don't you have any idea what I've done for you?'

'I have.' Carl Larson pushed his way to the fire. 'You risked your life when you could have played it safe. We're beholden to you, Horn.'

'Beholden?' Morgan spluttered. 'Why, Horn's tried to tell me how to run this colony from the day we left Fort Wallace.'

'You need some telling,' young Hancock said. 'Looks like we're in a fix.'

'We could have dickered with Vance!' Morgan shouted. 'If we can't go to Lost Valley, we could have settled on his grant.'

'No,' Horn said. 'He hasn't got a grant. There's some land on the Picketwire that can be bought, but it doesn't belong to any Rocky Mountain Land Company. Besides, if there is a grant company, it's probably having trouble. There'd be questions about any title they'd give you.'

'We came to settle Lost Valley,' Carl Larson said stubbornly. 'Before I take the word of the men who were here, I aim to see the valley.'

'And get ourselves shot...,' Morgan began.

'Maybe not. What we just saw proves to me that Jim Horn is a fighting man. If I ain't mistook, this calls for fighting. That right, Horn?'

'Looks like it,' Horn said, 'but if these men have actually settled the north end of the valley, you're in a tight and no mistake about it.'

'We came all the way...!' a woman screamed.

'Wait!' Larson shouted. 'Wait, now. There must be some way to handle this. How about it, Horn?'

Horn glanced at Morgan, sullen-faced and bitter with resentment. This had been his first real test, and he had failed miserably. There had been more talk than Horn had guessed, more suspicion of Morgan, more distrust of his leadership. 'No sense of me saying anything,' Horn said. 'Morgan doesn't want my advice.'

'*I'm* asking for advice,' Larson snapped.

'But Morgan's president of the colony.'

'I reckon the rest of us have some say about the way this colony is run,' Larson said angrily. 'Our constitution and bylaws provide for the president calling a meeting of the board of trustees when we run into an emergency, and I say this is an emergency.'

'I'm not calling a meeting of the trustees.' Morgan stood by the fire, facing the crowd, striving desperately to hold to his mantle of leadership. 'I started this colony. It was my idea from the beginning. Time and time again it has been proved that a number of people, working together, can do things an individual cannot. The Greeley colony proves it. Jim Horn does not believe in the very principle we stand for, yet you ask him for advice.'

Another man had moved up to stand beside Larson, a blacksmith named Fred Collins. Horn did not know him well, for he was a silent man who seemed capable of living within himself, but he had been respected enough by the colonists to have been elected a trustee. 'It is time for plain speaking, Angus,' Collins said. 'I believe your words hypnotized us or we would never have left Ohio. We're here now, and we can't go back. I believe we can make a go of this undertaking if we do the right thing. If we make a mistake, we're defeated. It is time for a meeting of the trustees.'

'We'll do the right thing!' Morgan cried. 'I promise you we will, but at a time like this it would be foolish to listen to this man.' He motioned to Horn. 'He owns nothing but his horse and his saddle and his long hair.'

They continued to stare at Morgan, their hostility a heavy pressure against him. Horn, watching them, sensed a dogged strength in them he had not felt before. What they had seen tonight had aroused in them something that had been dormant and had at last been awakened by this raw land. A few minutes before they had been afraid. Since then they

53

had been threatened, they had seen a man die in the violent manner that had been typical of the West since the days of its birth. Their distrust for Angus Morgan had crystallized, their faith in Jim Horn had grown. They were watching Jim, waiting for him to speak, hopeful that he could point the way for them.

Still Horn hesitated, realizing more than ever the depth of his love for Ruth and knowing how Angus Morgan would feel toward him if he were responsible for the man's removal from office. It was Ruth who forced Horn's decision. She walked toward him from where she had been standing beside the back wheel of the wagon, her head high. She put her arm through Horn's and faced the crowd, her back to her father.

'I think this talk about Jim's long hair is crazy,' she said. 'Long hair didn't hurt Samson.'

Angus Morgan was generous enough to laugh and say: 'I hadn't thought of that. All right, Horn. Speak up.'

'As I see this proposition,' Horn said slowly, 'there's just two things you can do. There's still good land to be bought along the Cache la Poudre and the Saint Vrain. From what I've heard, the Greeley folks are doing fine. The altitude is lower, and that makes the crop-growing season much longer.'

'That's a long trip from here,' Larson objected.

'And we'd have to buy the land,' Collins added.

Horn nodded. 'But it's railroad land, and you'll get a clear title. Or you can preëmpt government land.'

'We'd be there too late for a crop this year,' Larson said.

'That's right.'

'How much would it cost?'

'Oh, maybe four dollars an acre.'

Larson laughed shortly. 'And we want twenty thousand acres.'

'Which makes eighty thousand dollars,' Morgan said maliciously. 'Where are we going to get that kind of money?'

'What's the other thing we can do?' Rusty asked.

'Homestead in Lost Valley.' Horn hesitated, not wanting to say what was on his mind. 'Maybe we'd better sleep on it and decide in the morning just what we want to do.'

'We won't do no sleeping the way we feel,' Larson said. 'We'll have that trustee meeting first thing in the morning. You hear, Angus?'

'What good do you think it will do?' Morgan asked harshly.

'Four heads are better than one,' Collins said. 'Strikes me we made a mistake sending out a one-man locating committee.' Horn nodded. 'Webb's pulling out just before Vance and his bunch rode in doesn't look good.'

'Ike Webb is all right!' Morgan bellowed. 'I would trust...'

'We've heard that too many times,' Larson said angrily. 'Don't say it again. Horn, I've got one question that I want answered before we go to bed. Can we make the grade in Lost Valley?'

56

'I think so, but you'll have to fight. I don't see any way out of it.'

Larson nodded and turned away. 'Let's go to bed.'

Silently the crowd moved toward the wagons. Horn sensed the misery that was in them, the misery of people who have dreamed big dreams, and then have seen them fade. Now they must face brutal reality, but they were not shying away from it, as Angus Morgan had, and in that fact Horn saw some hope for them.

Horn remained by the dying fire, smoking, aware that Morgan had come to stand beside him. He did not look up, and presently Morgan said: 'I hired you for a guide. Nothing more. Now you have stolen my daughter and you have destroyed the faith my people had in me. I believe that gives me ample reason to kill you, Horn.'

Horn did not look up. 'Answer a question for me, Morgan. If Webb had been to Lost Valley, why did you need a guide?'

'He didn't know the route a wagon train

should take. He traveled horseback. We moved slowly, and we had to have grass and water.'

'There might be another reason,' Horn said.

'What?'

Horn gave him a direct stare. 'I don't think Webb ever came west of Pueblo. It's my guess he met Vance there, and they cooked this up.'

'You're crazy,' Morgan snapped. 'I've got everything staked on Ike Webb's honesty.'

'That's one of your mistakes.'

Morgan squatted beside Horn, and threw some wood on the fire. He said: 'They'll try to vote me out of office tomorrow. Maybe it isn't important, but there's one thing that is.'

'What?'

'Ruth's safety and her happiness.'

Horn studied Morgan for a moment in the firelight. It was a different Angus Morgan now, more humble and with the swagger and the sense of self-importance drained out of him. Horn said: 'She'll be all right.'

'I wish I could be that sure.' Morgan took

a long breath. 'I watched you kill that man tonight. It proved something I knew from the first. You're a savage, Horn. You wouldn't know how to treat a wife like Ruth.'

'She'll make her choice.'

'But it isn't a fair one. There's something about you that appeals to her. Your strength, perhaps. Or your talent for doing many things and doing them well. Or the ruthlessness that's a part of you. But whatever it is, I promise one thing. If you hurt Ruth, I'll kill you.'

'You should *if* I hurt her.'

Morgan rose. 'We understand each other?'

'I understand you,' Horn answered, 'but you don't understand me.'

'I think I do,' Morgan said. 'You can give the new president advice in the morning.' Morgan went on to his wagon.

Horn let him go. Words would be wasted. Angus Morgan would never change, but Horn had learned one thing about the man that surprised him. He loved Ruth more than he did himself. Horn rolled another cigarette, and smoked it, wondering what Morgan would do if they removed him from office.

Morgan and Rusty Hancock slept under the wagon, Ruth inside. Usually Horn made his bed by the fire, but a restlessness was in him tonight that he did not fully understand. It was not that he really expected an attack. Clay Vance would take a more roundabout way to accomplish what he wanted.

Tomorrow, Horn thought, Vance would try again. Perhaps he would make another attempt to sell a bogus land grant to the colony. Or he might make an offer for Travis and the rest of the settlers to withdraw from the valley for a sum of money. That would be no solution. The colonists would not be able to pay what Vance would ask, and it would not settle anything with Newt Kimmel.

Horn rose and made a circle of the camp, telling himself that his fears had no real basis. If Vance meant to force a deal, he would not attack the camp. Trouble would come in the cañon, if the colonists tried to reach Lost Valley, and it would be real trouble. A handful of men with Winchesters, hidden in rocks on the sides of the cañon, could hold back the entire wagon train.

There was no sound now from the camp except the sonorous snoring of tired and worried men. Horn returned to the fire, thinking he should try to sleep. Tomorrow would be a rough day. Still, he could not throw off the sense of danger. He rolled another cigarette, and put more wood on the fire, and thought of Ruth.

The decision would be his, and it must be made soon. It might hurt Ruth, but in the end she would forget him and marry Rusty who would give her a good home. It would be all right. He kept telling himself that, but all the time he knew he was wrong. No matter how far he rode, he would never forget. He was the kind of man who took one woman into his heart; she possessed all of it, and there was no room for another.

Yet there was Ruth's happiness to think about. He had been called half Indian. Morgan had just said he was a savage. Well, maybe it was true. Half true, anyway. He was a drifter, a man who refused to live by what most people called normal standards. His long hair and buckskins were marks of his independence. But in reality they were more than that. They were throwbacks to a former era when life had been filled with the daily adventure of grappling with the primitive forces of the wilderness. To Jim Horn's way of thinking, society was false and dishonest, a point Ruth would never understand.

Today Ruth had left no doubt of her feelings for him. It was strange, because all the way from Fort Wallace she had seemed friendly but no more than that. Thinking about it now, he wondered if she had been as distant as he had thought. Perhaps, as she had said, it was a man's place to do the pursuing, and she had not let him know how she felt until they had reached the time when he planned to leave.

A faint sound from the darkness penetrated his consciousness. Probably some animal searching for food. He looked around and saw nothing to alarm him. He heard Morgan's heavy breathing, saw the vague mounds under the wagon that were Morgan and young Hancock. He turned back to the fire, wondering why he was so jittery.

It came again, more definite and closer, the swishing of a man bellying toward him through the grass. He whirled, right hand reaching for his gun, and realized at once he did not have time to get it out of holster. Ike Webb came lunging out of the darkness, the firelight glittering on the naked steel of a knife in his hand.

Chapter Two

Horn did the only thing he could, for there was no time to pull his gun from leather. He fell forward on his face, a maneuver totally unexpected by Webb. Horn felt the blade rip through his buckskin shirt. He jumped up, threw Webb off, and scrambled to his feet.

There was time then to shoot the man, for Webb had fallen into the edge of the fire. He clawed frantically to get clear of the coals, cursing shrilly in pain, and in that instant a gunshot slammed into the night. Webb rolled over on his back and lay still, right hand flung out, the knife falling from lax fingers.

Rusty Hancock crawled out from under the wagon, a smoking gun in his hand. He shouted: 'I got him, Horn! I got him dead center.'

Horn restrained the fury that gripped him. A dead Ike Webb was not what he wanted. When he had dumped Webb into the hot coals, he had placed the fellow at his mercy. It had been his intention to beat the man until he talked. Now Webb had little time left for talking.

Horn dropped to his knees beside the stricken man, asking: 'Why did you want to kill me, Webb?'

The camp had come to life. There were shouted questions, lanterns bobbed here and there among the wagons, and a baby started to cry. Morgan came to stand over Horn, and Ruth, pulling a maroon robe over her slender body, had slipped out of the wagon. Rusty Hancock stared at Webb, the jubilation gone out of him. His eyes were fixed on the blood that made a dark stain on Webb's shirt, and only then did he seem to realize that he had killed a man. Turning, he stumbled to the river and was sick.

'Did Horn shoot you, Ike?' Morgan demanded. 'So help me, I'll hang him to the nearest tree.'

Horn rose and hit Morgan, knocking him back against a wagon wheel. He said – 'Stay there, damn you!' – and knelt beside Webb again. There was blood on the dying man's lips, small bright bubbles, and his face was gray. 'You haven't got long, Webb,' Horn pressed. 'If you want to clear yourself in hell, you'd better talk.'

'I'll be there ahead of you, Horn,' Webb breathed, 'and I'll blackball you. We'd have pulled this off if it hadn't been for you.'

65

Others crowded up, Larson and Collins and some more. Ruth was there, and now Morgan began edging back, one hand feeling gingerly of his jaw.

'We've got a lot of women and kids in this outfit,' Horn begged. 'If they starve to death this winter, it'll be on your head.'

Webb was going fast. His right hand was clutching his bloody shirt, his left clenched in agony. His eyes were glazed, the defiance gone now, and fear of the unknown was in him. He had enough life to whisper: 'Me and Vance ... were ... going ... to ... split ... the fifty ... thousand...' That was all. He shuddered, his right hand slid off his chest, and his mouth fell open. The vacant expression of death took possession of his face.

Horn rose and faced the crowd. 'Rusty woke up in time to see Webb try to knife me, and he let go with a shot.' He could hear Rusty beside the river, and he held back the rest of the things he wanted to say. The boy had done what he thought he should, and there was no use in condemning him for it.

Larson stared down at the dead man. 'I don't understand this, Horn. He said something about fifty thousand. You suppose he meant dollars?'

'He meant dollars all right.' Horn pinned his eyes on Morgan who stood in the inner circle of the crowd. 'Wonder how Webb knew that much *dinero* was in the wagon train?'

'There ain't,' Larson said in disgust. 'We're as poor as Job's turkey. Somebody sure fooled him.'

Morgan stared at Webb, shoulders slack. Watching him, Horn wondered what was in his mind. Stubborn as he was, and pinning his faith in Webb as he had, Morgan could no longer doubt Webb's guilt.

'Better go to bed,' Horn said. 'We'll plant him in the morning.'

They faded away into the darkness, muttering questions that could not be answered. The frightened baby whimpered, then it was silent, soothed back to sleep by the mother's soft singing. Horn, watching Morgan's grim face, wondered if the man was touched by those sounds, whether he even heard them.

Ruth stood alone, a slender dark shadow close to the wagon. Horn said: 'Get some canvas, Ruth. We'll wrap Webb in it.'

She brought the canvas, and Horn rolled the body in it and carried it away from the fringe of firelight. When he came back, Morgan and Ruth were standing beside the fire. It had died down until it made only a dull glow in the darkness. Horn could not see Ruth's face clearly, but he felt the tension that lay between the girl and her father, and he came to her and put an arm around her.

'Get some sleep,' he said. 'You'll need it tomorrow.'

She shivered, pressing close to him as if seeking strength from him. She asked: 'There'll be more trouble?'

'A lot more,' he said. 'I can't figure any way out of it.'

'Dad told Webb about the money, didn't he?' Ruth asked tonelessly. 'And Webb had sold out to Vance?'

'That's about it,' Horn answered. 'I figured

Rusty had just a dab, but fifty thousand is worth a heap of killing. Vance aims to have it.'

'Go to bed, Ruth,' Morgan said in a low, bitter voice. 'I have something to say to Horn.'

'There's nothing you can say now,' Ruth whispered. She walked to the wagon, and crept inside.

Horn threw more wood on the fire as Rusty came around the wagon, stepping over the tongue slowly as if he lacked the strength to go around it. He dropped to the ground beside the fire, his face very pale.

'I killed him, Horn,' Rusty said. 'I saw him and the knife, and I just shot.'

Horn knew the boy still did not realize the extent of the mistake he had made, and he could not find the words to tell him. He said: 'It's all right, Rusty.'

'But I killed a man,' Rusty breathed. 'You shot that fellow tonight and you didn't turn a hair. It was just like killing a prairie dog to you.'

'Webb needed killing. So did the man I

drilled, but don't ever plug the wrong man or it'll be on your soul as long as you live.'

Rusty looked at Horn in the fire light, sweat making a shine on his bony face. He said: 'Yeah, I guess Webb deserved it all right. What does it mean, Jim?'

'It means you're fetching a hell of a lot of *dinero* into a country like this,' Horn said bluntly. 'Morgan should have known better.'

'We need money to develop a new country,' Morgan said harshly. 'Don't condemn me, Horn.'

'Condemn you?' Horn gave a short laugh. 'I don't need to. You've done it yourself. Most fellows do a few good things to balance off the mistakes, but all you've written down in the book are mistakes.'

Morgan's fists knotted, and he took a step toward Horn. Lacking the courage to do what he wanted to do, he stopped, and wiped a hand across his face. He breathed: 'I've tried to do good for a lot of people, and I will if you let me alone.'

'I don't aim to let you alone. Yesterday I

was ready to take my pay and drift, but now I'm staying.'

'If it's Ruth you're staying for,' Morgan said in a low voice, 'I'll tell you once more you can't have her. I'll kill you first.'

Morgan would try. Meeting the man's eyes, Horn was sure of it. Morgan would never forgive him for knocking him down. Sometime he would make his try, if he had the opportunity, perhaps in the darkness or from the protection of brush or timber, or a boulder big enough to hide him. Angus Morgan did not have the courage that it took to fight in the open, but he was all the more dangerous because this was so. And he was Ruth's father.

'Maybe it's Ruth,' Horn said. 'Or Rusty's money that he deserves to keep. Or maybe it was the baby I heard crying a while ago. Did you ever think what winters are like in this country, Morgan, with hungry kids?'

'It was cold in Ohio,' Morgan said, 'and kids got hungry there. Out here they've got a chance to get their bellies full.'

'A mighty slim one. I reckon that's why I'm gonna hang and rattle.' Horn motioned wearily. 'Now go to bed before I beat hell out of you.'

Morgan wheeled back to his bed under the wagon.

Rusty said: 'I'll sit up, Jim. If I try to sleep, I won't see anything but Webb, lying there with my bullet in him.'

'Think of it this way,' Horn said. 'There never was a place in the West that was gentled down without some killings. That's our job. We've got to gentle down Lost Valley so these women and kids can live there and be safe.'

Rusty nodded eagerly. 'I want a hand in it, Jim.' He took a long breath. 'I've hated you from the day we left Fort Wallace because you've taken Ruth away from me. You didn't know it, but I did. Well, it's like you said this evening. If a man can't win a woman, he don't deserve her. I found out something else, too. I just ain't man enough for her.'

Horn rolled a cigarette and was silent, his eyes on the flames. He wanted to think of

Ruth and his love for her, of her kiss and the way she had clung to him, but the picture would not come clear. Angus Morgan was in the way. A man could not kill the father of the girl he loved – but he could be killed by him.

They sat there that way until the camp stirred to life with the first drab light of dawn. The wood was gone. Horn took an axe and, with Rusty trudging beside him, moved upstream to a dead cottonwood and began chopping. He was bone-tired when he drove the axe into the limb, then the weariness dropped away from him. This was something to do, something physical that for the moment took his mind off Angus Morgan, and he felt the better for it.

Horn cut more wood than Ruth needed for breakfast. Other men were chopping around them, and he motioned for some of the boys to help themselves to the wood he had cut.

Presently Larson moved over to him, asking: 'What are your plans, Horn?'

'I'm going into the valley right after the burial.'

'You'll need help.' Larson sleeved sweat from his face. 'I didn't sleep none after the shooting. Kept thinking about the money Webb said was here. Must be in the wagon train or it wouldn't be working like this. You know, Vance riding in last night and wanting to sell us land on the Picketwire.'

Horn chopped a limb in two and, straightening, leaned on his axe. He asked: 'Larson, how well did you know Morgan before you left Ohio?'

'Not real well. He had a newspaper in a town about fifty miles from where Sadie and me lived. Times were bad and I was out of work. Morgan came around, signing folks up for this colony, and, well, we'd heard about the Greeley colony. Morgan made it sound good. He's right persuasive, you know. Uses big words real handy.'

Horn nodded, knowing how it had been. Larson was like the rest of them, little men reaching for the rainbow that Morgan painted for them. The hell of it was that Morgan really wanted to help. It was probable that he honestly hoped to take young Hancock's money and double it for him, out here where money was scarce and opportunities were waiting like ripe plums to be picked from a tree.

'Better have breakfast,' Horn said. 'We've got a job of burying to do.'

It was Horn and Rusty and Collins who dug the grave close to the base of the hill. It was Larson who made the marker and carved Webb's name on it. They gathered around the grave, all the colonists, including the children, and Morgan read from the Bible. Then, lifting his face to the morning sky, he prayed. He knew big words, Horn thought, and he used them well. If Horn needed proof of Morgan's talents, he had it here, in this simple service.

They lowered the body into the grave, and the people moved back to their wagons, all but the men who remained behind to fill the grave. Morgan walked across the grassy flat to Collins, saying: 'We'll have the meeting now.' He looked at Horn, hating him with his eyes. 'You want to sit in on the meeting?'

'No. I ain't a member of your colony.'

'I had the impression that you thought you were,' Morgan said evenly.

'Then you're making another mistake,' Horn said, and swung away toward his horse.

Horn saddled his black gelding and rode to the river. He loosened the cinch, and stood there while his horse drank, unaware that Larson had come to stand behind him until the man said: 'What do you hope to accomplish in this valley?'

Turning, Horn looked at the man's broad grave face. He said: 'I ain't sure, but I want to see if Travis and his bunch really have settled the valley.'

'Is it safe for us to try going up the cañon?'

'Hell, no. They'll pick you off like sitting ducks on a pond.' He tightened the cinch. 'I rode for a fellow named Newt Kimmel who used to have the only ranch in the valley. Newt came here when the Utes were thicker'n flies, and he stuck it out. Claimed the whole damned valley. I figured he'd be the one who'd give you trouble.'

'You think he might help us?'

Horn shrugged. 'Newt is no hand to help any batch of sodbusters, but there's something fishy about this deal. It isn't like him to let Travis and this outfit settle the valley.'

Larson scratched his nose, the corners of his mouth jerking. He said: 'Horn, I'm scared worse'n the day I got married, but this is our fight a lot more'n it's yours. I'll go along.'

'Thanks, but I'll do better by myself.'

Relieved, Larson nodded. 'Well, we ain't got a pretty job on our hands, voting Morgan out of office.'

'There's one thing you've got to make 'em savvy.' Horn stepped into the saddle. 'You folks came from a country where you could call a sheriff or a policeman when you got into trouble. Out here there is no law except what you make with your Winchesters.'

'I'll get it through their heads,' Larson promised, 'if I have to pound it in with a hammer.'

Horn rode upstream, keeping his eyes straight ahead. He did not want to talk to Ruth this morning. She might get it into her head to go with him. He splashed across Lost Creek, spread thin here in the gravel beside the river, and fifty yards farther west began angling up the steep south wall of the cañon.

It was slow going through the cedars, and Horn made frequent stops to blow his gelding. An hour after he left the river, he found a deer trail and by mid-morning had reached the top. Lost Valley lay before him. For a long moment he sat his saddle, thinking again, as he had thought many times when he had ridden for Newt Kimmel, that if he had to settle down in one place for the rest of his life, he would pick Lost Valley over any other spot he had ever seen.

To the west the Sangre de Cristo range raised gaunt granite peaks thousands of feet above the floor of the valley. Here and there patches of snow remained, defying the sun. Far to the southeast he could see the Spanish Peaks, made hazy by distance. Pike's Peak was visible to the northeast. Directly to his left were the ragged, pine-covered foothills of a lower range, and there, he knew, was fine grama grass and range as good as a man would find anywhere.

Lost Valley was a cowman's paradise. He could not blame Newt Kimmel for marking it as his own. Kimmel had held it against other cattlemen and against settlers. It seemed unreasonable that Ben Travis and his bunch could have successfully defied Kimmel. They would not have remained a week when Horn had ridden for Clawhammer.

Horn turned his gelding southwest. From here he could not see the Clawhammer buildings, but they were not far from him. He would reach them by noon, and he would know the answer to the question that had been plaguing him since Clay Vance and the others had ridden into camp the night before.

Lost Valley was too big and too good for one man to hold indefinitely, a fact of which Kimmel had long been aware, but he'd told

Horn many times that he'd hang on as long as he could. Meanwhile, he'd be home-steading the best part of the valley. His headquarters were on the north fork of the creek, a low, well-watered section of the valley carpeted with blue joint and wild timothy that furnished good winter graze. During the summers his cattle were driven up into the spruce and aspens on the shoulders of the Sangre de Cristo range or into the pines to the east.

Newt Kimmel had never been one to consider death. Or if he had, there was his daughter Dixie to think of, a red-headed tomboy that Horn had been certain would never grow up. He remembered her as a fiery-tempered kid with pigtails down her back and a brain that could think up more deviltry than any boy Horn had ever known. She would be eighteen now, and Newt close to fifty. It was hard to picture Dixie that old, and even harder to think of Newt being middle-aged, but time never stood still. There would come a day when Jim Horn would be middle-aged. He wondered sourly if he would still be wearing buckskins and long hair just to prove that he had not surrendered to an encroaching civilization that had already brought steel rails to Denver and plows that were turning the sod of thousands of acres along the Cache la Poudre and the St. Vrain.

Silly! Just plain damned silly, one man standing against a powerful current. He could hate this thing people called progress, but he couldn't hold it back any more than Newt Kimmel could keep his grip on Lost Valley. Jim Horn was outmoded; he might as well get a haircut and admit it. They would come, the farmers and the blacksmiths and the carpenters, the Carl Larsons and the Fred Collinses and the Rusty Hancocks. Yes, and the Angus Morgans and the Ike Webbs and the Clay Vances. The solid men and the riff-raff.

If Horn had been as true to his principle as he had thought, he would never have guided the colony from Fort Wallace. But there had been a woman in the beginning, he had not thought of it that way, but he was honest with himself now. He loved Ruth Morgan, loved her enough to forsake his principle of giving no help to those who brought what they called civilization. If he had held unalterably to that principle, he would have gone on and let Vance and Travis rob the colonists, let Morgan fail as a man with his conceit was bound to fail.

Horn came into an open spot atop a ridge and reined up. He looked down upon the Clawhammer buildings, but he saw them only with his eyes. Something had become clear to him that had never been really clear before, even though he thought it had. He had reached the point at last where he must surrender. Ruth Morgan meant that much to him. He thought of Rusty Hancock's money and the good that could be done with it here in the valley. He thought of the child he had heard crying during the night and its mother's lullaby. They were wrong when they had called him half Indian and a savage. If he had been, he would have ridden on as he had planned. There had been a day when a man could control his life, but that day was gone. He had been blind or he would have seen it a long time ago. He had not wanted to see it. That was the whole truth of it.

He lifted his reins to ride on when he heard a shout. He hipped around in his saddle, right hand reaching for his gun. Then it fell away, and he swore softly. Ruth and young Hancock were riding up the ridge, Ruth waving to him. Then they were out of sight in the scrub oak, and he sat there, waiting, a cold rage growing in him. The thing he had wanted more than anything else was to keep Ruth out of danger.

It was another fifteen minutes before they emerged from the brush and rode up beside him, Rusty's face bleeding from where a limb had slashed him, Ruth's blouse torn under her left arm.

'Don't get mad,' Ruth said the instant she could be heard. 'You had no right to ride off without saying anything to us.'

You had no right! He stared at the girl, weariness from the hard ride showing in her face, then he looked at Rusty who was dabbing at the cut on his cheek. A moment before Horn had been telling himself he had reached the point where he would surrender. Now rebellion rose in him. It was a hell of a thing when a man couldn't ride out of camp without being followed and told what he didn't have the right to do.

'Yeah,' Rusty said. 'Damn it, Jim, you can't take all the risks. It's our fight more'n it's yours.'

'You shouldn't have brought Ruth,' Horn said hotly. 'I don't know what I'm headed into.'

'But you wouldn't have headed into it if it hadn't been for me,' Ruth said. 'You'd have gone on and you'd have been safe by now. Don't you see?'

'Go on back.'

She shook her head, lips tightly pressed. 'No.'

Rusty shifted uneasily in his saddle. 'It ain't that we're just tag-alongs, Jim. Ruth said she had to come, and I couldn't let her come alone.'

'You left your money...?'

'Nobody in the colony will steal it. Seemed like the thing for me to do was to give you a hand.'

He looked at the girl, and then at Rusty. They thought they were right. They thought they could help him. He could not bring himself to tell them they'd be in the way, that whatever he had to do he could do better by himself.

'Come on, then,' Horn said brusquely. 'I'm going to the ranch yonder. Won't be any trouble there, I reckon.'

He rode down the slope, Ruth on one side of him, Rusty on the other. They reached the creek that curled slowly between willow-lined banks, crossed it, and came up to the south side, horses straining in the mud before they achieved solid footing.

'I think it's magnificent,' Ruth said in a

low voice. 'It's the most beautiful valley I've ever seen.'

'Clay Vance thinks so, too,' Horn said, his voice still brusque.

'A man could raise grain here,' Rusty said. 'Don't seem so dry. Plenty of water to irrigate with if we have to, and there's timber for our sawmill. Looks good to me.'

Good if they could fight and hold it, Horn thought, but he killed the temptation to put it into words. Instead, he said– 'Short growing season.' – and let it go at that.

Ten minutes later they reached the Clawhammer buildings. There was no change here, Horn thought. The same sprawling log house shaded by ancient cottonwoods, the barns and outbuildings, the pole corrals. It was as if he had left only yesterday.

'You know, Jim,' Rusty said, 'I always had a notion I wanted to be a cowboy. What's the chance of getting a job here?'

Horn did not answer. Ruth was looking at the mountains, at the fresh pale green of the aspens and the black fingers of spruce that reached high up on the steep slopes, then she tipped her head back to stare at the gray granite that lay above timberline. She said reverently: 'Jim, I guess every human being dreams of finding God's country. I believe we have.'

Horn said nothing to that. He had more important things to consider than Rusty's wanting to be a cowboy or Ruth's finding God's country. Something was wrong here. The ranch seemed deserted except for the horses in the corral and the thin pillar of smoke rising from the chimney. Ordinarily there was a good deal of activity around the ranch. Now there was no sound to indicate human presence. He wasn't sure, for he had seen Vance's and Travis's horses at night and at some distance from the firelight, but he had a feeling that the bay and the roan geldings in the corral belonged to Vance and Travis.

'We've got trouble,' Horn said in a low tone. 'Rusty, pull your gun and leave it in front of you. Don't get squeamish if you have to kill another man.'

Rusty hesitated, eyes whipping to the house and coming back to Horn's grim face. He asked: 'What's wrong?'

'Dunno, but aim to find out.' Horn stepped down, catching the blur of someone's face behind a window in the ranch house. He called: 'Hello, the house!'

The front door slammed open, and a girl ran down the path, red hair streaming behind her. 'Jim! Jim Horn!' It was Dixie Kimmel, grown up and almost as tall as Ruth. When Horn had seen her last, she had been a child.

Dixie kissed Horn and hugged him with the fervency of a woman who has just had a prayer answered. Then she brought her mouth close to his ear, her arms still around him. She whispered: 'Don't come in.' She drew back and looked at him.

He put a finger against her pug nose, grinning at her. 'You turned out to be quite a woman. I never thought you'd make it.'

She stepped farther away. 'And I thought you'd have a haircut the next time I saw you. Still playing mountain man?'

'Naw. Aren't enough mountains no more. Just can't afford to go to a barber. I've taken to playing guide for a wagon train.' He motioned to Ruth. 'Dixie, this is Ruth Morgan. She belongs to the train, and she thinks this here valley is heaven. Ruth, this is Dixie Kimmel. Her dad owns Clawhammer.'

'How do you do,' Ruth said, her voice cool.

'Sure glad to know you, ma'am,' Dixie said, 'only Dad doesn't own much of anything these days. And you're plumb wrong about this valley being heaven. It's a chunk transplanted from hell.'

'She was just a kid when I rode for her dad,' Horn said. 'As ornery a brat as I'd ever seen. Dixie, the long drink of water yonder that didn't get the Lord to dye his hair as red as yours is Rusty Hancock. Says he wants to be a cowboy.'

Rusty lifted his hat. 'Pleased to know you,

Miss Kimmel.'

'Howdy,' Dixie said. 'I'm right sorry, but we aren't taking on any hands right now.'

'Who's in there?' Horn asked.

Dixie bit her lower lip, frowning. Then she said: 'A couple of no-goods named Clay Vance and Ben Travis. They're killers, Jim. Get back on your horse and ride off like you'd just dropped by to say howdy.'

'Vance?' Ruth whispered. 'Travis? What does it mean, Jim?'

'I'm wondering,' Horn said. 'Newt alive?'

'Yes, but that's about all. Go on now, Jim. Ride off, or there'll be hell to pay.'

'Why, now,' Horn said softly, 'it just happens we have something to settle with those *hombres*. Rusty, don't go off half-cocked, but keep that iron of yours handy.'

'Jim, you can't...,' Dixie began.

'Got to,' Horn said, and, stepping past the girl, walked through a patch of shade to the house. He shouted: 'Vance, you still got that grant on the Picketwire?'

Vance stepped through the door to the

porch, as dudish and immaculate as he had been the night before. He put a hand on a porch post, smiling with cool confidence. 'That I have, bucko. Change your mind about taking it?'

'It's worth talking about. Where's Travis?'

'In the house. Why?'

'I want to see him.'

Vance tipped back his white Stetson and scratched his head. 'Your business is with me, friend, if you want to settle on the grant.'

'I've got a question to ask Travis. Call him out.'

'What question?'

'I had an idea after the ruckus last night. Your outfit didn't look like farmers to me, so I got the notion that maybe you and Travis heard we were coming and saw a chance to sell something.'

Vance unbuttoned his coat, exposing a short-barreled gun in a shoulder holster. He looked past Horn at Ruth, smiling amiably. 'You're riding in bad company, Miss Morgan.'

Ruth rode toward the house, worried eyes touching Horn's face briefly and swinging back to Vance's. She said: 'It could be worse.'

Vance laughed. 'I don't take that kindly. I like beautiful women, Miss Morgan, especially if they have spirit. You know, women are like horses. If a woman is like a plow horse, she's no fun. No fun at all.'

Horn made a half turn so that he could watch Vance and still see Rusty and Dixie who remained on the other side of the cottonwoods. He motioned for Rusty to ride up, knowing that Travis was inside and that he probably had a gun in his hand.

Jim Horn had been in some tight spots, but none as tight as this. There was a chance to play it through, but it was not a good chance, for it depended on Rusty Hancock. If the boy blew up too soon, Jim Horn was a dead man.

'I don't take kindly to being compared to a horse, Mister Vance,' Ruth said coolly.

Vance laughed again, softly, with the confidence of a man who is sure of himself. 'I'd call it a compliment, miss. It depends on the horse, of course, and the woman. I never ran into a horse I couldn't ride, or a woman I couldn't tame.'

'You won't tame me,' Ruth said, her chin thrust forward defiantly, 'if that's what you're getting at.'

'I'll take that bet,' Vance said, 'and give you odds. I'm a right good hand with women, and with your dad running that bunch of greenhorns I hold good cards.'

'Damn you!' Rusty shouted.

'All right,' Horn cut in. 'Call Travis out, Vance. We've had enough palaver.'

Irritated, Vance said: 'I'm talking to the lady, long hair. She'll make a deal with me, and her dad will take it. I'll give odds on that, too.'

'Then you'll lose your bet,' Ruth said. 'When we left camp this morning, the trustees were having a meeting. By now my father has been voted out of office.'

Vance frowned, and his gaze shuttled back

to Horn. 'That right?'

'I think so,' Horn said. 'Morgan's made too many mistakes. Webb was one of them. Now are you gonna call Travis out?'

'What kind of offer do you figure to make Travis?' Vance asked.

'I had a notion he'd pull out for a price ... with his friends.'

'They might at that. Ben, come out here.'

Travis appeared, a Colt in his hand. He stood there, a blocky man almost as wide as the doorway. He said: 'I don't like the smell of things, Clay. We ain't heard from Ike.'

'You won't either,' Horn said. 'You had it fixed for him to cut me up like a Christmas turkey, didn't you?'

'That was the idea,' Travis agreed.

'I killed him,' Rusty called out. 'I've got you covered, Travis. Drop your gun.'

Vance stiffened, his eyes swinging to Rusty as if this was a twist in the game he had not expected. Horn did not turn. His right hand was close to his gun butt. He said: 'Vance, I'm guessing you're right handy with that iron you're toting. Now if you feel lucky, try your luck.'

Vance shook his head. 'I had my stack bet on Webb, and I saw what happened last night. I'm holding a good hand without taking any chances on dying.'

'You're looking at the bright side of this,' Horn said. 'The kid's a good shot. He plugged Webb in the brisket.'

'It doesn't matter,' Vance said. 'My boys are in the cañon. Anybody who tries to get a wagon into the valley is a dead pigeon. You'll settle nothing here.'

'I'll settle Travis if he don't drop that gun!' Rusty shouted. 'I'm scared. I'm so damned scared my finger's getting tight on the trigger.'

Vance said: 'Drop your iron, Ben. He might do it.'

Travis let his gun go, cursing. 'I told you I didn't like the smell of this.'

Horn, watching the big man, made up his mind. Vance was the smart one, Travis the bully. Without Travis, Vance could be handled. Horn did not know how much depth there was to Ben Travis, but there was a good chance that, if he was badly beaten, he could be bluffed into leaving the country. At the moment it seemed the only way to play it.

'I reckon you put Webb up to knifing me, Travis,' Horn said evenly. 'Come down off that porch. I aim to beat hell out of you.'

For a moment Ben Travis didn't move. His shoulders hunched up until his ball of a head was indrawn like a frightened turtle's, but Travis wasn't frightened. His tiny eyes, deeply recessed in their sockets, showed surprise, and then they began to glow with anticipation. A moment before he had thought the gun in Rusty's hand was enough to beat him, but now a new hope throbbed in him.

Behind Horn, Dixie cried: 'Don't do it, Jim. He'll beat you to death.'

Travis stepped down from the porch, walking slowly, great arms at his sides.

Horn said: 'Watch Vance, Rusty. Keep him out of this.'

Dixie cried out again, her voice panicky:

'Don't do it, Jim. Nobody has licked Travis since he's been here.'

'He's getting a licking now,' Horn said.

It was Horn's guess that Travis was an expert at barroom fighting, the kind where no rules held. He'd butt with his head, he'd knee a man, he'd ram his thumbs into a man's eyes if he got him down. But Horn had done his share of that kind of fighting. He could take care of himself if Vance was kept off his back. That was his one worry as he moved in, driving his first blow into Travis's hard-muscled body.

Travis took the blow without so much as a grunt and lunged forward, trying to get his hands on Horn. Reach was on Horn's side, bull strength on Travis's. So Horn was faster than the big man, but knowing, too, that one mistake would be a fatal one.

The ground was uneven and deep with dust. If Horn stumbled, it would be the break Travis was counting on. For a time Horn fought carefully, keeping out of Travis's reach, slashing him across the face and hitting him in the chest, continually moving, while the dust stirred and rose around them.

There was no sound from the watchers. Vance smiled slightly as if there could only be one way for this to end. Rusty, his nerves as taut as overly tight fiddle strings, kept his eyes on Vance. Ruth was bending forward over the saddle horn, her face pale. Dixie was clenching her fists and swinging them with each blow Horn landed, her whispered – 'Give it to him, Jim. Damn him, give it to him.' – not even reaching Ruth's ears.

There was only one way to fight Travis: until the man was worn down, or irritated to the point where he left himself wide open. Horn held rigidly to that plan, slashing out with lightning fists, rolling his head and making Travis miss by a fraction of an inch when he threw a punch, or taking it on his elbows or a shoulder. All the time he was giving Travis brutal punishment. He chopped a right to Travis's nose and brought a stream of blood; he drove a left to the man's chest, a right to the eye. Between flurries he backed away until he had become familiar with every inch of the ground underfoot.

'Stand still and fight,' Travis panted. 'Damn your yellow hide.'

Horn taunted him with a laugh. 'You're hittin' nothing but air, mister.' Coming in close, he rocked Travis's head with a vicious right.

Horn's plan was paying off. Not so much in the slow wearing down of Travis's great strength, for most of Horn's blows were slashing rapier thrusts that did little more than sting or cut. If it kept going this way, Travis would outlast him, for Horn had spent a sleepless night and was beginning to feel the slowing down that came from bone-deep weariness. But he was making Travis frantic in the way a mosquito does that bites and gets clear from a man's slapping hand to return and bite again. Sooner or later Travis would give way to fury.

Horn's opportunity came sooner than he expected. Travis threw a swinging right that started at his heels. It missed and threw him off balance, and Horn drove in and knocked him down. Travis fell face forward into the dust. He came up at once, coughing and spitting and cursing, and dived headlong at Horn.

Horn stood there, refusing to give ground, and brought his knee up squarely into Travis's face. The blow was perfectly timed. The *crack* of it was like that of a descending butcher's cleaver slamming into a side of beef. Travis's head snapped back on his short neck. Horn stepped aside as he fell.

This time Travis was slower to get to his feet. His wide face was a mask of sweat and blood and mud. He shook his great head as if the ability to think had been knocked out of him. There was a chance he was faking, but it was a risk Horn had to take.

Now Horn moved in fast. He brought his right through to the side of Travis's head, his full weight behind it. Travis's knees buckled, and his hands came down as he fought to hold himself upright. As he began to sag, Horn hit him once more with a powerful fist flush to the point of his bearded chin. This time Travis lay still when he fell.

Horn stumbled to the porch and sat down, wiping his face with his hands. He said: 'Thanks, Rusty. I was afraid you'd take your eyes off Vance long enough to let him get his gun out.'

'I watched him all right,' Rusty said shakily, 'and I was kind of hoping he'd go for his gun. Seems like our trouble would be over if he was dead.'

Dixie had come to the porch, trembling a little. She breathed: 'You should have killed him. You ought to kill Vance. You ought to hang both of them.'

'I'm hoping this will do the job.' Horn motioned to Vance. 'Saddle up. Take Travis and get out of the valley.'

Vance laughed softly. 'Well, my friend, you're tougher than Ike Webb allowed you were, but you haven't done the job. We have legally filed on our homesteads, and we will stay.'

'I killed one of your men last night,' Horn said, 'and you've just seen what I've done to

Travis. You're too smart a gambler to play your hand out.'

'We'll see,' Vance said. 'We'll see.'

Travis was getting up, still dazed, blood drooling down his face from a dozen cuts. Vance moved past him to the corral.

Horn said: 'Go with 'em, Rusty. Keep 'em covered till they ride out.'

Horn sat there, wiping sweat from his face until the other two had saddled and mounted. Then Vance called – 'Don't make the mistake of thinking we're finished, Horn!' – and rode off, Travis behind him, swaying drunkenly in his saddle.

'I may have busted my hands up,' Horn said. 'Got some hot water, Dixie?'

'Sure have.' Dixie looked at Ruth. 'Come in, Miss Morgan.'

'Take care of our horses, Rusty,' Horn said, and followed Dixie into the house.

Ruth stepped down, giving her reins to Rusty who had ridden up, and went inside. Horn sat down at the kitchen table and began soaking his hands in a pan of hot water that Dixie brought to him. He looked at Ruth, grinning wryly.

'Sorry you had to see that, Ruth.'

'I don't understand.' Ruth dropped into a chair across the table from Horn. 'You forced that fight, Jim. Why?'

'I can tell you why he did,' Dixie broke in as if irritated. 'There's some folks you can argue with, but there's others you've just got to knock some sense into their heads. Jim was working on the same notion that Travis did when his bunch came to the valley. Travis opened up a saloon in his cabin. Our boys got to going down there, and Travis picked fights with a couple of them. Almost killed them. Soon as they could ride, they drew their time.'

Horn flexed his hands, rubbed them, and put them back into the hot water. 'Travis wouldn't pull a gun on me, Ruth. Using my fists was the best I could do. I'm hoping he'll pull out now.'

'Might work,' Dixie said. 'He's been al-mighty proud of his fighting, so maybe he'll tuck his tail and run now that he's lost his reputation. Or he may hang around and try to dry-gulch you.'

'What's been going on hereabouts?' Horn asked.

'Trouble!' the girl cried. 'Nothing but trouble for the last six months. Vance's bunch settled on the creek. Vance offered to buy us out, about ten cents on the dollar. Dad laughed in his face. Then somebody dry-gulched Dad. Got him in the chest and he almost died. You won't know him, Jim. He just doesn't look the same.'

'Can he talk?'

She nodded. 'We've had the doctor from Canon City. He left some stuff to give Dad so he sleeps most of the time, but when he wakes up, he can talk your leg off.'

Horn lifted his hands from the water, clenched them and opened them several times, and nodded as if satisfied. 'Didn't hurt 'em none, I reckon.' He walked to the stove and took a towel down from a nail on the wall. 'What about your crew, Dixie?'

'What crew?' she demanded. 'We don't have one. Chuck, Marty, and Jake were dry-gulched. Two more were beaten up like I told you. The rest took their time and left the country. We haven't had a man on the ranch for a month.'

Understanding how the girl felt, Horn nodded. Newt Kimmel had never kept as big a crew as he should have. He'd always said there was no sense wasting money on cow-hands' wages when there wasn't another spread within fifty miles, so he had depended on a few good men who had been with him for years. They were the ones who had been dry-gulched, and the rest, drifters who would not give their outfit the loyalty a good rider does, had sloped out of the country.

'What about your cattle?' Horn asked.

'I've done what I could,' she said miserably, 'but it wasn't nearly enough. They're scattered from one end of the valley to the other. We've lost some. I can't prove it, but I'm dead sure Vance's bunch has rustled several hundred and sold them in the mining camps where nobody cares what brand a beef's got on it.' She turned away. 'We're busted, Jim. Busted flat. I tried to get to Pueblo to hire a crew, but Vance won't let me out of the valley.'

'Maybe some of our men could help,' Ruth said.

Dixie whirled on her, saying: 'How much good would a...?'

'How about dinner,' Horn broke in.

Dixie turned back to the stove. 'I'll get it, Jim.'

'Newt asleep?'

Dixie nodded. 'It'll be evening before he wakes up.'

'What was Vance doing here today?'

'More of the same. Trying to get me to sell. Dad would sell the place if I said so.'

Ruth got up to help Dixie, and Horn walked into the living room. For a time he stood in front of the stone fireplace, massaging his hands and thinking that this room had not changed in appearance since the first time he had seen it. The crude furniture that

Newt Kimmel had made when he'd settled in the valley, the guns on the walls, the bear rugs, the battered melodeon that had been freighted in from Denver – it was all as he remembered it.

It was essentially a man's room. Some women would have changed it but Dixie had left it the way Newt liked it. Perhaps she didn't know how to change it, for she had been raised in a world of men. Her mother, Horn recalled, had died the first year they had been here.

Rusty came in, looking at Horn with new respect. He said: 'That was sure a hell of a fight, Jim. You cut him down like he was a pine tree.'

'Maybe wasted,' Horn said bitterly. 'I didn't know how the land lay, or I'd have done it different. I should have killed both of 'em like Dixie said.'

Dixie called – 'Dinner!' – and they went into the kitchen. They ate in silence, Horn's mind on Clay Vance. It was plain enough what the man was after. He wanted the gold that was in the wagon train, but that was incidental. His main object was to get Clawhammer. That explained why he didn't want the colonists in the valley. They might help Newt Kimmel, and that was the one thing Vance could not allow, not when he was this close to getting what he wanted.

When Horn finished, he pushed back his plate, and rolled a smoke. He said 'I want to talk to Newt. Maybe Ruth's idea wasn't so bad, Dixie. After we trim Vance down a little, I think we can work out a deal so Newt won't kick about the greenhorns coming into the valley.'

'He's not in shape to make any kind of deal,' Dixie said dully, 'but you can talk to him this evening when he wakes up.'

Horn rose. 'I think I'll hike back to the river. Ruth and Rusty will stay here.'

'What are you going to do?'

He grinned at her. 'Well, now, I ain't just sure. I'll see how the voting went.'

'I'm going back with you,' Ruth said:

'No, you won't. You're done sashaying

around over the valley. You're staying right here if I have to hog-tie you.'

She frowned, fighting an impulse to argue with him. Then she said meekly enough: 'All right, Jim.'

'I'll fetch Collins and Larson back with me so they can have a powwow with Newt.'

'Jim.' Ruth had gone rigid, her eyes on the window. 'Larson's coming.'

Wheeling, Horn ran out of the house, Rusty behind him. Larson was riding up the creek as fast as he could make his jaded horse travel.

Dixie cried: 'Look at that fool. He's killing his horse.'

Horn ran across the yard and past the cottonwoods, knowing that something was wrong or the man wouldn't be riding that way. Larson reined up, his face grim.

'There's hell to pay,' Larson said through dry lips. 'Morgan talked better'n I thought he could.'

Horn reached up and gripped his arm. 'What happened? Damn it, talk.'

'They kept Morgan in as president, and he persuaded them to try coming up the cañon. He's driving the first wagon.'

Ruth cried: 'He'll be killed! He will be, won't he, Jim?'

There were many things Jim Horn could have said about Angus Morgan. This was defeat, the very move Clay Vance wanted the colonists to make. Once driven back down the cañon, they would not try again.

Horn thought then with a sense of guilt that he should have foreseen this. He knew the depth of Morgan's stubborn pride and he knew how well the man talked. But he said none of the things he wanted to say. There was no use hurting Ruth now. She would be hurt enough later on.

'I reckon he will,' Horn said, 'unless we can fetch him a miracle. Let's saddle up, Rusty.'

Chapter Three

It took valuable minutes to rope a Claw-hammer horse and change Larson's saddle to it, and to throw gear on Horn's and Rusty's horses. Horn carried a Winchester in his scabbard, but Larson and Rusty had only their belt guns. Horn reined up in front of the house and asked for rifles. Dixie brought them at once with several boxes of shells.

'Dad always said there wasn't any sense to putting money in a bank,' Dixie said. 'He claimed the best investment a man could make was in guns and ammunition.'

She handed the .30-30s to Rusty and Larson. Horn's eyes turned instinctively to Ruth, standing on the porch in the trim, proud way she had, her shoulders back, her head high. She was able to give Horn a small smile and wave to him. It seemed to

Horn in that short moment, when he tried to fill his eyes with the sight of her, that he had never loved her as much as he did now.

'Don't you worry, Ruth,' Rusty said. 'They'll be all morning getting harnessed up. We'll probably get to the cañon ahead of them.'

It wasn't true, and Ruth knew it. She said – 'Good luck.' – and Horn, watching her, sensed that it was all she could say without losing her self-control.

The three of them rode down the creek, Horn turning once to look back. He raised a hand to Ruth, then they made a turn, and the house was lost to sight behind a screen of willows. It occurred to Horn, as it had so often, that only a freak of nature could have made it possible for Angus Morgan to have sired a girl like Ruth. But freak of nature or not, she was his daughter, and she loved him.

Larson glanced at Horn, his face grim as if expecting Horn's fury to fall upon him. Finally he burst out: 'I couldn't stop 'em Jim. Damn it, I tried, but I ain't a talker like

Morgan. It wasn't just the trustees. Morgan was too smart for that. He said this was for everybody to decide, so he called in all the men. He made a speech, and they went down the line for him.'

'I thought everybody was against him,' Horn said.

'Hell, they was, but I tell you Morgan's got a tongue. Should have gone into politics. He allowed we'd never see you again. Said you didn't have a nickel invested in the colony and you wasn't the kind to settle down with 'em, so you wouldn't give a damn what happened.'

'Why, the crazy...,' Rusty began.

'I know, I know,' Larson broke in, 'but we wasn't sure you and Ruth would find him. Morgan's big argument was that every day counted. He said we had to get crops in if we wanted to eat next winter. When you get right down to brass tacks, I guess that was what's been worrying everybody more'n anything else.'

'It's too late now,' Horn said. 'Won't be

113

easy breaking sod up here.'

'They didn't know that,' Larson said. 'What they wanted was a look at the valley. Morgan said if it didn't pan out good, they'd have a talk with Vance about his grant on the Picketwire. Morgan figured that Vance was bluffing about not letting anybody come up the cañon. He convinced 'em mighty quick when he said he'd take the first wagon. The women and kids are walking behind so they won't get hurt.'

'That's more sense than I thought he had,' Rusty muttered. 'The hell of it is my money's in his wagon.'

'We'll get it back for you,' Horn said.

Rusty grinned. 'I think you will, Jim. Damned if I don't think you can do anything.'

'You could have stopped 'em if you'd been there,' Larson said, 'but I couldn't. When Morgan starts talking in that way of his, folks forget what they said about him yesterday, and they won't remember till it's too late.'

'If it wasn't for Ruth,' Rusty said bitterly,

114

'I'd hope Angus gets it between the eyes. It's like I told you, Jim, I lived beside him, and I knew he was big talk and little do, but I came along just the same.'

'How'd you find us, Carl?' Horn asked.

'Luck mostly. I seen the way you started. Followed your tracks long as I could. I lost 'em, but, when I got to the top of that ridge yonder, I saw the ranch and figured it was the best bet.'

Horn nodded. There was no more talk for a time, and presently they reached the junction of the two forks of the creek. At this point the stream turned north, dropping quickly into the cañon. There was a cabin here, and Horn could see several more up the south fork, small log buildings with dirt roofs. There was no sign of life around them, no gardens or chickens or pigs, no ground broken by the plow. It proved what Horn had been sure of. Clay Vance and his bunch had never intended to stay and farm.

'Where do you reckon Vance and Travis went?' Rusty asked.

'Hard to tell,' Horn answered.

'You figure they're around somewhere?'

Horn shrugged. 'They might be drawing a bead on us now. Depends on how Travis took his beating. Vance may have trouble making him stay in the country.'

They heard the first shots then, directly north and not far down the cañon. Horn wheeled his horse at once, nodding to the others, and rode along the west rim, keeping above the cañon that broke off sharply below them. The creek was a shining silver ribbon at the bottom, the road beside it little more than a boulder-strewn trail.

'Better get down there, hadn't we?' Rusty shouted.

Horn shook his head, calling back: 'No! We've got to stay above 'em.'

Ten minutes later they saw the first wagon. Morgan's, Horn guessed. It was lying on its side at the edge of the creek, both horses dead. Morgan would be somewhere around. He was probably dead, too, although he may have had strength enough to crawl into the brush. Stubborn to the point of being foolish, and bound to have his way, there could be no denying the peculiar kind of courage that had been in the man. He had not been able to face Jim Horn with a gun in his hand, but he had boldly flouted Clay Vance's order by bringing his wagon on ahead of the others.

Horn reined up in a thicket of scrub oak and, pulling his Winchester from its scabbard, stepped down. He had heard spasmodic firing from Vance's men, but he doubted that any more damage had been done. He judged they were throwing lead to warn the colonists more than anything else.

The cañon made a bend directly below Morgan's wagon, and from where he stood on the rim Horn could not see any of the others. Apparently Morgan had come some distance ahead of the second wagon, and the rest had stopped before they had come into rifle range.

Rusty and Larson had dismounted.

Horn said: 'We'll tie here. They won't be looking for us to buy into the fight.'

'Angus is a goner,' Larson muttered, 'or I'm mistook.'

'Keep low,' Horn warned. 'We don't want 'em to spot us. We've got to get the rest of the wagons up before dark, or it'll be a hell of a bad deal.'

Rusty said something under his breath. A man halfway down the cañon had fired a shot. He was directly below them, his head and shoulders visible. Rusty brought his Winchester to his shoulder, and, when Horn batted the barrel aside, saying – 'No.' – Rusty wheeled, fury boiling through him. 'What the hell,' he breathed. 'It'd be like shooting fish in a barrel.'

'It's a little more than that,' Horn said. 'Just how brave are you, kid?'

The fury died. Rusty sleeved sweat from his face. He said: 'I ain't brave at all, Jim. Why?'

'I'm working on a notion. I think we can get those wagons up.' The firing had stopped, and except for the one man below them there was no sign of life on either side of the cañon. Horn scratched his cheek thoughtfully. 'You see, there isn't room for the wagons to turn around, and they can't back down. We've got to get 'em up.'

'I don't see how,' Larson said. 'Hell, these devils can sit there all day.'

'They know where your money is, Rusty,' Horn said. 'Chances are Morgan told Webb, and Webb told Vance. Come dark, they'll move down and take Morgan's wagon apart.'

'And we sit here and watch them do it,' Rusty said tonelessly.

Horn shook his head. 'Not if you want to be bullet bait. Soon as another wagon shows up, they'll start shooting. If Larson can spot 'em, he can make it damned hot for 'em.'

'Where you gonna be?' Larson asked.

'Busy.'

'Bullet bait.' Rusty shook his head. 'Don't sound like fun, but I'll do it.'

Horn grinned. 'You'll do it, kid. Tell the rest to string along behind you. Won't take you more'n half an hour to get down there to 'em.'

'It wasn't like this in Ohio,' Rusty said.

'Tell Ruth I...'

'You'll be around to tell her yourself. Take it on foot and keep undercover.'

'I don't like it,' Larson said. 'I'll go, Jim.'

'You've got a wife and kids. Don't drive from the seat, Rusty. Walk on the right side of the team and stay close to 'em. First shot you hear, get under the wagon.'

Rusty said – 'I'll sure do that.' – and started into the cañon.

Horn waited until the boy had disappeared, then he turned to Larson. 'Stay here. If I'm doing this wrong, you'll have to shoot straight, or they'll nail Rusty.'

'What are you up...?' Larson began.

But Horn had already slipped down the slope, moving swiftly and quietly through the brush, careful not to start a rock rolling down the steep slope. He could still see the man that Rusty had started to draw a bead on. The fellow was lying motionless behind a boulder, attention on the turn in the cañon.

Horn did not know how many men Vance had, but it was a reasonable guess that the six he had brought into camp the night before was all of them. Collier was dead. It was not likely that Vance and Travis would be here. That left three, and, judging from the amount of firing Horn had heard when it started, that number would be about right.

It took fifteen minutes of careful maneuvering to reach a point above the rifleman. Here a sandstone ledge ten feet high ran along the side of the cañon parallel with the rim. A number of boulders lay along the edge with, here and there, a few runty cedars that gave scant cover. For most of the fifteen minutes Horn had been unable to see the man. If he changed position, Horn's plan would fail. If one of the others spotted Horn, he'd be a dead man and his plan would certainly fail.

Reaching the ledge, Horn bellied across it, entirely in the open now and visible to anyone above him. His spine began to prickle. He should have told Larson to shoot any of Vance's men who showed themselves above him, but it was too late now.

He eared back the hammer of the Winchester as he eased between two boulders. The man below heard the click and whirled as Horn's head appeared over the ledge.

'Stand pat,' Horn ordered.

'The long hair,' the man breathed. 'You damned sneaking Injun.'

'I think I'll lift your scalp,' Horn said. 'Your yeller hair will look good in my teepee.'

Sweat beads popped through the skin of the man's face. He wet his lips, staring at Horn as if expecting a bullet any minute. Horn remained silent, letting fear work through the fellow.

'Go ahead,' the man breathed. 'Why don't you shoot me?'

'I decided I'd lift your scalp while you're still alive,' Horn said as if he had given it careful thought. 'Then I'll let you go. When Vance and Travis get a look at your noggin, they'll tear out of the country like bats out of hell.'

The last bit of restraint left the man. He began to beg, his hands clasped in front of him.

Horn laughed contemptuously. He said:

'You sure look comical. Where'd Vance find anything like you? What's your name?'

The man's flabby lips sagged open. He whispered: 'It's D-Dyer. What do you want?'

'How many men are in the cañon?'

'Three.'

'Where?'

'There's two of us on this side. One on the other.'

Horn swore softly. That made it bad. He had hoped all of them would be on this side and that his prisoner could call them in. He asked: 'How far away is the one on this side?'

'Right below me.'

'Can he hear you?'

The man nodded.

Horn said: 'Call him up.'

'Suppose he don't come?'

'Why, I reckon I'll have me a yaller-haired scalp.'

'I'll try.' The man gulped and repeated: 'I'll try.'

'First thing you'll do is drop your gun belt over yonder with the Winchester. I'm not coming down to have a look see, but if you've got a hide-out on you and you make a try for it, I'll blow your brains out.'

The man unbuckled his gun belt with trembling fingers and tossed it toward the Winchester. Then he shouted: 'Meeker. Come up here, Meeker.'

The man below called: 'What'n hell do you want?'

'They're sending some men up the cañon. Can you see 'em from where you are?'

'No.'

'Then get up here with me. Looks like a hell of a lot of 'em. Regular damned army.'

'What's the matter with your eyes?'

'Nothing. I'll need help picking 'em off, that's all.'

Grumbling, Meeker clambered up the rocky slope and presently appeared through the brush a few feet from Dyer. He growled: 'I don't like the smell of this a little bit. Vance and Travis ought to be here. If them greenhorns start to rush us...' Then he saw Horn and stopped, mouth dropping open.

'That's fine, Meeker,' Horn said. 'Keep coming. Lay your Winchester and your gun belt with Dyer's on the rock.'

The man obeyed, cursing Dyer in a bitter voice.

Dyer said defiantly: 'He was gonna lift my hair. I couldn't do nothing. How'd I know he'd Injun up on me?'

'Didn't help none to pull me into it!' Meeker shouted angrily.

'What about Morgan in the lead wagon?' Horn asked.

'I got him with my first shot,' Dyer said. 'He fell out of the seat and crawled back into the brush. Ain't seen him since.'

'Where's your third man?'

Meeker motioned across the cañon. 'Over yonder. He couldn't hear us if we hollered at him.'

'Then we'll go after him,' Horn said. 'Were I you, I wouldn't try to warn him or make a run for it.'

To Horn's right the ledge broke off in a rock-strewn slant. Horn drew back and slid down it. There was a moment when either Dyer or Meeker could have safely made a dive for one of his guns or jumped into the brush and got clear, but their backs were to Horn and they didn't have the opportunity until it was too late.

Horn, two steps behind them now, said: 'Head for the creek.'

They made a slow descent, both Meeker and Dyer being careful not to give Horn an excuse to shoot. They reached the road beside the creek, and Horn, uncertain whether the man on the east side of the cañon could see him or not, stepped behind a cottonwood.

'Now, it's up to you boys to fetch your partner down here,' Horn said.

Meeker and Dyer swung to face him. Dyer started to whine, and Meeker cuffed him across the side of the head with an open palm, saying: 'Shut up. That ain't gonna get you nothing with this *hombre*.'

'That's right,' Horn said. 'I'm running out of time and patience.'

'Damn it,' Meeker said bitterly, 'we can't do what we can't do. Benson's too high up to holler at.'

Horn had not realized how nearly the time he had given Rusty had run out. Now he heard the *clatter* of a wagon and his eyes turned downstream, quick fear knifing through him as he realized his scheme was not working, and that he was likely to be the cause of young Hancock's death.

Horn saw the wagon, and in that same instant the man above him cut loose with his Winchester. Meeker, taking advantage of Horn's shift of attention, grabbed for a gun in a shoulder holster. Horn had a glimpse of Rusty, diving under the wagon. Then he heard the report of a .30-30 high up on the western rim and knew that Carl Larson had located the man across the cañon.

Everything seemed to happen at once, too many things for Horn to grasp at the moment, but he caught the motion of Meeker's hand as he went for his gun and barely had time to swing his rifle from Dyer to Meeker and fire. Meeker stumbled forward and fell. He rolled over once into the creek, and lay still.

Dyer started to run downstream toward Rusty's wagon.

Horn yelled: 'Hold it!'

Dyer, panicky now, began to zigzag in a frantic effort to escape. Horn let go with a shot that kicked up gravel at his feet. Rusty, still under the wagon, cut loose with a shot that caught Dyer in the neck. He went down in a headlong fall, and Horn, running behind him and coming up to him, saw that he was dead.

Rusty scrambled out from under the wagon, and began to talk to his horse and pull on the lines. Horn dropped his rifle, and took hold of the bridles, helping Rusty quiet the horses, aware that he was making a fair target for the man on the cliff above him. Both Larson and Vance's man had stopped firing, but that might not mean anything. As soon as the team quieted down, Horn moved back beside Rusty.

'I killed another man,' Rusty said bleakly. 'I keep trying to remember what you said. About men like these needing killing.'

'You're saving the county hanging money.' Horn put a hand on the boy's shoulder. 'A man wouldn't want a better partner, kid. I was plenty worried there for a minute that I'd got you into something.'

'Hell, you were into something, wasn't you?'

Horn shrugged. 'I'm used to it. What kind of a shot is Larson with a Winchester?'

'He's a good shot. We all did some hunting back home. I guess we wouldn't stack up with you when it comes to pulling a six-gun, but when we've got time to aim, any of us would do pretty good.'

Horn looked up at the brushy east side of the cañon. 'Wish I knew about that *hombre* up there. Just the three of 'em and we sure as hell fixed these two. Funny thing what a man will do when he gets boogery. That Dyer fellow never should have run. No sense to it.'

There was silence for a moment. Horn

was still studying the east side of the cañon, when a faint voice called: 'Horn! You out there, Horn?'

'Morgan,' Rusty whispered. 'He's over yonder. In the brush.'

Wagons were coming upstream now, and Horn was still not sure about the man above him. He hesitated, knowing that he could not reach Morgan without coming into view of the rifleman above him, but he judged that Morgan had been hard hit or he would not have called like that. Horn lunged toward him, bending low, and dived into the brush, expecting a shot that did not come. He bellied toward the wounded man, keeping a screen of willows between him and the road.

Morgan lay on his back, eyes closed, a dark bloodstain on his shirt. His face was pale, so pale that for a moment Horn thought he was dead. He crawled forward until he was beside Morgan, and felt of his wrist.

'I'm alive,' Morgan whispered, 'but I won't be long. Where's Ruth?'

'She's at Clawhammer. She's safe.'

'Keep her safe, Horn. I'm giving her life into your hands. I would not have done that a few hours ago. I had planned to kill you.'

Morgan's eyes were still closed. His pulse had been a faint throb, so faint that Horn had had trouble finding it. Horn sat motionless, saying nothing. He could not think of anything to say to a man who had hated him as Angus Morgan had, and who now was dying.

'I've had time to think about a lot of things,' Morgan went on. 'I knew I was a goner and there was no one to help me. I wanted to talk to Ruth, but it's all right now that I know she's safe. Tell her I love her, Horn. Just tell her that.'

'I'll tell her.'

'Queer how a man's values change when he gets to the place I am. I've been a failure, Horn. You seemed to know that the instant you signed on with us. I'm a failure whose only talent was with words. I trusted Webb, and I thought I had to go on trusting him no matter what you said.'

Morgan was silent, and Horn thought he was gone. Then he opened his eyes and tried to see Horn. Failing, he closed them again. He breathed: 'The light's out. Won't be long, so I've got to hurry. I'm going to ask something of you. I never thought I would. Stay with the colony, Horn. They need you. Will you promise me that?'

Jim Horn possessed his share of weakness. He had made his mistakes and he'd had his failures, but he had never gone back on his word. If he gave it now to a dying man, it would be doubly sacred. He hesitated, hating this man who, waiting at the portals of death, wanted to bind his future.

'Perhaps someday you will understand how it has been with me,' Morgan whispered, 'always striving for something I could not attain. First it was for my wife, and then for Ruth. Now you've got to do what I wasn't big enough to do. Promise me, Horn.'

Dry-lipped, Horn said: 'I'll do what I can.'

A moment later Morgan was dead. Horn rose, and stood looking down at him, wishing he could have known Ruth's mother.

When Horn got back to Rusty's wagon, two others had come up behind it and stopped. Fred Collins, walking upstream toward Rusty, saw Horn and called: 'Is it safe to move up now?'

'I think so,' Horn said. 'There's one yahoo up yonder I'm not sure about. I'll go see to him.' He motioned to the brush where Morgan lay. 'You'll have to elect a new president.'

Rusty and Collins were silent for a time, both looking away from Horn as if they felt they should say they were sorry and could not bring themselves to do it. Then Collins muttered: 'Too bad for Ruth.'

'Yeah, she's gonna take it pretty hard.' Rusty pinned his eyes on Horn. 'She's sure gonna need you now.'

'I'll be around,' Horn said.

Picking up his rifle, Horn waded across the creek. Larson, almost down the west slope, called: 'I got that fellow up there, Horn! Spotted him as soon as he cut loose at Rusty.'

Horn swung up the slope, angling to the

south. He wanted to be alone as much as anything. He thought of the promise he had made Angus Morgan and wondered if he could do anything for these people. It depended on several things – and on Ruth, and the colonists, and on their chance of success. Too, there was his own future to consider.

There was this pulling and hauling within him, his love for Ruth on one hand, and on the other his fear that it would be wrong for him to marry her. As Rusty had said, he'd take her to 'hell-an'-gone and she won't have nothing.' He knew himself, knew his inherent sense of rebellion against authority and the accepted standards of a settled life. So, because he loved her, he was afraid to marry her. He wondered if other men found only misery in a matter that should make them happy.

He found the body of the man Larson had shot and turned back down the cañon. He reached an open space, and stopped on a sandstone ledge to smoke a cigarette, idly watching the men below him as they righted

Morgan's wagon. They brought another team up, and Rusty climbed into the seat.

Wagons rolled up the cañon, dust boiling around them. Women trudged along the road. Kids played in the creek, chasing each other and slipping on wet rocks and tumbling in to get soaked head to foot. A moment before there had been danger. Now it was over, and the children had forgotten it. It was too bad, Horn thought, that a grown person had lost so much of the ability to forget.

There was nothing for Horn to do until camp was made and a meeting called. Clay Vance, he knew, could not be counted out. Men like Collier and the three who had been killed today could be hired by the dozen in Denver or Pueblo or Trinidad. Vance had been too close to success to quit now. He might leave the valley, but he would be back. Besides, there was Ben Travis.

Horn went down to the creek and crossed it, stepping between two wagons. He nodded at the driver of the one below him and climbed the west slope. Rusty's and Larson's horses were still here. Horn untied them, mounted his gelding, and, loading the other two, rode south along the rim until he reached the head of the cañon. Rusty, he saw, was bringing Morgan's wagon up the last steep pitch. The others were strung out behind him as far as Horn could see down the cañon, a weaving line of weathered canvas tops.

'Jim."

It was Ruth's voice. Horn hipped around in his saddle, surprised to see Ruth and Dixie coming toward him from the cabin at the forks. He saw the question in Ruth's eyes, and looked away. He would have to tell her. She came on toward him, and, when he brought his eyes to her again, he was surprised to see the composure in her face.

'He's gone, isn't he?' Ruth asked in a low tone.

Horn nodded. 'I was with him when he died. He said to tell you he loved you.'

She bowed her head, fighting to hold her calmness of spirit. Horn waited, sitting motionless in the saddle, wanting to comfort her, to help her through these hard moments, but not knowing what to say or do.

Ruth raised her head to look across the valley at the towering Sangre de Cristo range. 'We'll bury him here, Jim. No matter what happens to the rest of us, he'll be here forever. That would be a victory for him, wouldn't it, Jim?'

'Yes,' he answered. 'He died a brave man, Ruth. He took the lead wagon and kept the others behind him so they could stop before they got into rifle range. That's why no one else was hurt.'

'A brave man,' Ruth said softly. 'He would like to know you had called him that.'

Then Jim Horn knew he could not hate the memory of the man who had bound him with a promise. Angus Morgan had had his weaknesses, but he had had his strengths, too, and they had been easy to overlook. The colony would never have reached Lost Valley if it had not been for him.

'We'll camp here tonight.' Horn motioned

toward the grassy flat that lay between the forks of the creek. 'We'll have a palaver after supper.'

'Have you seen Vance or Travis?' Dixie asked.

Horn shook his head. 'We got the three that were in the cañon. Two of 'em were called Dyer and Meeker.'

'I know them,' Dixie said. 'The third one was Benson, but they're just small fry. Nobody's safe as long as Vance is alive.'

'Newt?'

'Still asleep when I left. He'll be waking up about dark.'

'You staying here?'

Dixie glanced at Ruth who was walking slowly toward the Morgan wagon that had reached the top and was rolling on toward the flat between the forks. 'For a while, Jim. She can't keep that stiff upper lip forever.' Dixie gave Horn a searching look. 'She's got more to her than any greenhorn woman I ever saw. She's your kind.'

'I ain't sure I'm hers,' Horn said. He was

silent for a moment, watching the wagons roll over the crest, and grinned when a man yelled: 'Hooray for Lost Valley!' Horn swung his gelding toward the wagon behind Rusty, calling back: 'I'll tell Larson to keep an eye on things! I'll get Rusty, and we'll go have a talk with Newt.'

'I wish you would,' Dixie said. 'I don't like leaving him alone.'

Larson had taken the wagon that Rusty had been driving, and, as Horn rode toward it, he heard Rusty tell Ruth: 'Both of your horses were shot. We had to pull another wagon over to the side and put the team on yours.'

'Dad?'

'He's inside. Don't look at him. Won't do no good.'

Horn was out of earshot then and reining up beside Larson who was leaning forward in the seat, a wide grin on his lips. 'Well sir, we kind of fixed Mister Vance's boys, now, didn't we?'

'But Mister Vance isn't fixed.'

Larson scratched his head, the grin dying

on his lips. 'No he ain't. Well, I see you brought our horses up. You must have done more walking today than you've done for a spell.'

'Reckon I have Carl, I've got a notion that this is the time to settle what you folks are gonna do. Rusty's got about all the *dinero* that's in the train, hasn't he?'

Larson nodded. 'Fact is, he's got all of it. I didn't know he had it till Webb let it out. Morgan must have aimed to use it to get us started, and I guess Rusty figured on letting him.'

'Before Morgan died,' Horn said, 'he made me promise to stay with the colony.'

'Well, now, that's good. Dunno what we'd have done without you.'

'That promise holds till you're on your feet, and I've got an idea for putting you there. Rusty and I are taking a ride. You run things while we're gone. Roll the wagons into a circle and put guards out. Watch the stock. You'll be in a hell of a fix if Vance runs off your horses.'

'We'll do it,' Larson promised.

Horn rode on to the Morgan wagon, leading Rusty's horse. Ruth was still standing there. Rusty had stepped down from it and was talking to her. When Horn rode up, the boy turned to him.

'She wants to bury him here,' Rusty said.

Horn nodded, thinking that in time there would be a town here called Morgan City and Angus Morgan would become a legend, his failings forgotten, his values magnified. He glanced down at Ruth who was still holding her composure, and he thought it would be better if she let herself go and cry.

'Dixie's gonna stay with Ruth,' Horn said. 'Rusty, I figured you and I would ride back to Clawhammer.'

'All right,' Rusty said, puzzled.

'Don't go sashaying around, Ruth,' Horn said.

She nodded, but said nothing. Horn glanced up at the sun that was low over the mountains, jerking his head toward Clawhammer, but Rusty still hesitated. He put a hand out to Ruth and dropped it as if uncertain what to say.

'Go on,' Ruth whispered. 'I'm all right. Dying isn't so bad, you know. I mean, that's the way we have to look at it. It's just that Mother went a long time ago, and I haven't had anybody but Dad for so long.'

'You have me and Jim...,' Rusty began.

'Of course, I have,' she said quickly. 'Go on with Jim, Rusty. Hurry before I start to cry.'

Horn touched the brim of his Stetson and reined away. A moment later Rusty came up beside him, saying: 'I guess there's nothing that makes a man feel as worthless as having someone you love lose someone she loves. I can't feel real sorry about Angus, but Ruth...'

'She'll be all right,' Horn broke in. 'I don't know about things like that, neither, but Morgan showed more guts dying than he ever did living. I've got the notion that if you and I do what we've got to do, the colony will be all right, and that'll please Ruth because I'm guessing this colony was the biggest thing her dad ever tried.'

'What have we got to do?' Rusty asked.

'First I want to know if you've really got that fifty thousand in the Morgan wagon?'

Rusty nodded. 'In gold. It's in a false bottom that I rigged up myself.'

'How'd you come to have that much *dinero*?'

Rusty scowled. 'Hell, that ain't none of your business.'

'It isn't for a fact, but if I take you to talk to Newt Kimmel, I aim to find out if there's any strings attached to that *dinero*.'

'No, it's mine. My dad was pretty well fixed. Had a store and some other property. After he died, Morgan talked me into turning everything I had into cash and coming along. I told you I figured Ruth...'

'I remember,' Horn said impatiently, 'but there's some other things I don't know. Morgan aimed for you to invest in the valley, didn't he?'

'Yeah, he wanted to build a town out here and I was supposed to be the banker. Loan my money till everybody got on his feet.

We've got a gristmill and a blacksmith...'

'I know all that. Now I'm gonna put it up to you. If you don't give these people some help before winter, they'll be starving by spring. You still want to invest in the valley?'

'I dunno,' Rusty said gloomily. 'I've lost Ruth, but I ain't begrudging it. I mean, after seeing what you've done.' He shook his head. 'It's kind of hard to say, but you and Ruth go together like sugar and cream. If you'll settle down...'

'Damn it, we aren't talking about me and Ruth. Before we get to Clawhammer, I want to settle one thing. What are you gonna do with that fifty thousand?'

Rusty was silent a moment, his eyes on the Sangre de Cristo range, granite peaks set against the scarlet sky like giant saw teeth. He looked south at the valley with its green grass and willows along the creeks and, then hipping around in the saddle, looked back at the eastern hills touched with the sharp light of the dying sun. He came around slowly, a hand raised to rub his bony face.

'It's a pretty valley,' he said. 'I've got a hunch our people will make out. I'll see it through, Jim.'

'That's fine,' Horn said. 'I reckon you'll be that banker Morgan was talking about.'

They rode in silence until they reached Clawhammer. The sun was down by the time they dismounted. 'I'll see if Newt's awake yet,' Horn said, and went into the house. A moment later he returned. 'We may have to sit a while. Newt didn't look like he'd ever wake up. He's lost fifty pounds since I last saw him.'

They watered and fed their horses, and went into the house, Rusty lingering in the doorway until Horn had lighted a lamp. Horn carried it into Kimmel's bedroom, motioning for Rusty to follow. The Claw-hammer owner lay in bed, a single quilt pulled over him. For a moment Horn stood by the bed, holding the lamp, his eyes on the man, feeling again the paralyzing impact of shock just as he had a few minutes before when he had stood there.

Newt Kimmel had always been a tall, long-boned man, honed down to hard muscle by constant riding, but now he seemed to consist entirely of skin and bones. His face that had been deeply bronzed by wind and sun had faded to a ghastly gray.

As Horn turned to the bureau and set the lamp down, Rusty said: 'Hell, he don't look like he'll live till morning.'

'Dixie figured he was getting along,' Horn said. 'I reckon he'll be around for a while. Pretty damned tough, Newt is.'

Horn pulled a rawhide-bottom chair to the head of the bed and sat down. Rusty dropped into a chair on the other side of the room. They sat there for a time, smoking, glancing occasionally at the sleeping man, while outside purple dusk left the valley and night moved in, a pressing blackness relieved only by faint star shine.

'I thought Dixie and Ruth would be along before now,' Rusty said worriedly.

'Probably stayed in camp,' Horn said.

There was silence again except for Kimmel's light breathing. Presently he stirred and opened his eyes. He stared at Horn a long moment, blinking, then he said: 'Sometimes I see things when I wake up that ain't here, but damned if I don't believe you're really Jim Horn. Nobody else, either in this world or hell, could look as much like Jim as you do.'

'It's me,' Horn said, and held out a hand. 'How are you, Newt?'

'Slicker'n goose grease.' Kimmel pulled a skinny hand out from under the quilt and shook Horn's. 'The only thing that's wrong is I just ain't worth a damn no more.'

'Newt, meet Rusty Hancock from Ohio who wants to be a cowboy and has got more guts in him than any greenhorn I've ever seen before.'

Pleased, Rusty stepped up and shook Kimmel's hand. 'Glad to know you, Mister Kimmel. Don't let Jim fool you none. I've been scared ever since I left Fort Wallace.'

Kimmel's thin lips stretched into a grin. 'I sure cotton to an honest man. I'm scared, too, kid.' He gripped Rusty's hand and dropped it. 'What's more, I'm busted. When I get out of this damned bed, I start from scratch. Hear that, Jim? From scratch, and just last Christmas I bragged to Dixie I was the best fixed man in the territory.'

'You still are.'

'Like hell. Didn't Dixie tell you?'

'Sure, but Collier's dead. So's Dyer and Meeker. Another fellow they called Benson. Just Travis and Vance are left.'

'And Travis is beat all to hell,' Rusty said. 'Jim done it.'

The thin lips pulled back into the grin again. 'That's good news, but, as long as Vance is alive, I've got trouble. A slick one, that *hombre*. Anyhow, Clawhammer beef is scattered from here to breakfast. This valley is fifty miles long and ten wide, and most of them cows are up in the mountains by now. Why, even if I had a crew...'

'We'll gather 'em for you, Newt.'

'You and the kid? Jim, I used to tell you that your long hair would sap your brain and that's just what you've let it do.'

'Listen to me, Newt. I've got quite a yarn.' He told Kimmel about the colony and what had happened. He finished with: 'You've always claimed all the valley when you never used a tenth of it. Well, these folks are here. They'll build a town. They've got the fixings ... sawmill, gristmill, blacksmith shop, carpenter's tools. Everything. Horses and seed for farming. It'd be a good deal for both of you if you'd give each other a hand.'

'So help me, Jim,' Kimmel said angrily, 'I'd have to be worse off than I am to throw in with a bunch of greenhorns. Anyhow, I haven't even got enough *dinero* to buy grub...'

'I forgot one thing, Newt. Rusty here has fetched fifty thousand dollars in gold that he aims to invest in the valley. That means a loan to you. Now the settlers won't hurt you none. You've got all the grass on this side of the valley that you'll ever need, and you know it.'

Kimmel was silent, fighting his natural dislike of settlers. Then he said: 'Kid, if you've got that kind of money, you'll light out for the mines...'

'No, I won't. I like this valley.'

'Maybe you like Dixie.'

Rusty glanced at Horn. Then he nodded. 'Maybe I do.'

'Well, Jim,' Kimmel said bitterly, 'I ain't in no shape to augur.'

'I want your word that you'll help 'em,' Horn said. 'Sell 'em beef to eat this winter. Tell 'em what'll grow and what won't. Tell 'em where the best timber is. Best place for a dam so they can build a reservoir this summer when they can't do anything else but put up their cabins and maybe get in a late garden.'

'Jim, I thought you said this wasn't a good valley for farming,' Rusty said.

'It isn't, but there's a few grains that'll do all right. Hay. A few vegetables, but some things...'

'What you're trying to say,' Kimmel broke in, 'is sooner or later the settlers will get around to raising cows.'

'That's it,' Horn admitted. 'I always

claimed there was room for fifty ranches if you had neighbors you could get along with.'

Kimmel raised a hand and scratched the sharp point of his chin. 'Yeah, I remember what you said. Well, I wouldn't be listening to you if Vance hadn't showed up with a bunch of toughs and put a slug into my brisket. All right, Jim, I'll make that deal if you'll run Clawhammer till I get on my feet. With a loan from the kid I can make out...'

The beat of a horse's hoofs came to them. Whoever was coming was riding hard and fast. Horn ran out of the room to the front door. He stopped there, listening.

Rusty came up and would have gone on out if Horn had not held him back. He said: 'Let's see who it is.'

'It's trouble or...'

'Sure, sure, but we might live longer if we see who's fetching it.'

The horse was close now, a vague shape in the night. Then the rider pulled up under the cottonwoods, and Dixie cried out in a ragged voice: 'Jim! Jim, you there?'

'You bet I'm here,' Horn answered, and ran across the yard to her.

She swung out of her saddle and came to him, her hands gripping his arms. 'I ... I...'

She began to cry, and Horn shook her roughly.

'What is it?'

'Vance got Ruth. We were on our way back and didn't know he was waiting for us. Tied me up. I just got loose a few minutes ago. Came as fast as I could.'

'Where is he? What does he want with Ruth?'

'He's taking her to the Temple cabin. Said if you wanted her back, you'd come and get her. Said you had to be alone and you had to bring fifty thousand dollars.' Her finger dug into his arms. 'He said if you tried any tricks, he'd take her over the mountains with him and you'd never see her again.'

Chapter Four

Jim Horn had never been one to let emotion rule him. Like most men who'd lived the kind of life he had, he had been forced by circumstances to accept danger philosophically, to realize that death comes but once and that, when a man chooses the frontier, it might come any time even when there is no reason to expect it. But the threat of danger to himself and to Ruth Morgan were two different things, and now fear was in him. It started deep in his belly and flowed upward into his chest until it hurt with dull, pressing pain.

Rusty lashed out at the girl. 'Why in hell didn't you stay in camp...?'

'Shut your mouth,' Dixie flared. 'You're just a wet-eared kid. Shut up now.'

Whipped into silence, Rusty held his tongue.

Horn, shaking off the first shock, asked: 'What about Travis?'

'I didn't see him. He might have been there, though. Vance pulled me off my horse, and I scratched him. He hit me and knocked me silly for a while. When I came to, he had me tied up.'

Horn knew where Temple's cabin was, high up in the aspens on the slopes of the Sangre de Cristo range. He had been there many times when he had ridden for Clawhammer. Originally it had been a miner's shack, but Kimmel had worked it over until it was tight and sound and had used it for a summer cow camp.

Ruth would be comfortable and safe if it were any man but Clay Vance, but Vance could not be judged by the standards that applied to most Western men. Horn remembered how Vance had looked at Ruth the night he had ridden into the colonists' camp on the river and had called her 'a fair woman to find in such a country.' Horn was remembering, too, what Vance had said just before Horn's fight with Travis, about never having run into a woman he couldn't tame. Ruth had said: 'You can't tame me.' Those words, Horn thought, would be the kind of challenge Vance could not resist.

'Saddle my horse, Rusty,' Horn said. 'There's a lantern out there by the gate.' He wheeled toward the house. 'Come on, Dixie.'

'Now what the hell are you...?' Rusty began.

'Damn it, get a move on!' Horn called back. 'Saddle your horse after I'm gone. You've got another ride to make.'

Horn did not see if Rusty obeyed. Dixie caught up with him, asking: 'What have you got in your head, Jim?'

'I'm going after her. Where's that Thirty-Two you used to have?'

'In my room, but it's too small...'

'Get it. Fetch some string, too.'

The instant they stepped into the house, Newt Kimmel called: 'What is it?'

'Nothing to fret about,' Horn answered. 'Dixie's here.'

'I'm all right, Dad,' Dixie said, and ran into her room.

Horn lighted a lamp, took off his coat, and untied his neckerchief. When Dixie brought the little pistol and string, he checked it, saw that the pistol was loaded, and looped the string through the trigger guard. 'Drop it down my back,' Horn told Dixie, 'Tie the string so the gun will hang between my shoulder blades.'

She obeyed, understanding then what he had in mind. Now, with the lamplight fully upon her face, he saw the dark bruise on the side of her jaw where Vance had struck her, and fury worked through him like an all-consuming fire. He held his silence, and, when she was done, he re-tied his neckerchief and slipped into his coat.

'How does it look?' Horn asked, stepping away from her. 'See anything?'

She moved around him and shook her head. 'It's not enough of a bulge to notice unless you're looking for it.' She took a long breath. 'But Vance will be looking, Jim. He was a gambler in Pueblo. He'll know all the tricks.'

'Maybe he won't know this one,' Horn said, and left the house.

Dixie stepped into the bedroom, said something to her father, and ran after Horn. When she caught up with him, she said: 'Let me go with you, Jim. Rusty can stay with Dad.'

'No.'

'But Travis will probably be with Vance. I can shoot. Don't you remember how well I can shoot?'

But Horn ignored her question, and they went on to the corral.

Rusty had saddled Horn's gelding, and now he swung to Horn, bony face dark with worry. He said: 'I'm going with you. Don't tell me I can't. Ruth means...'

'I know how you feel, but this job's mine.' Horn put a hand on the boy's shoulder. 'When Morgan died, he said he was giving Ruth's life into my hands. Now I've let this happen.'

'Hell, it wasn't your fault.'

'I pegged Vance wrong,' Horn said grimly, 'and that was my fault. I just didn't think far enough ahead. I should have because I saw the way he looked at her.'

Rusty leaned against a corral post, shocked by a new fear that had not occurred to him before. He said in a low voice: 'I didn't think about him wanting Ruth. Figured he was after my money.'

'He wants Ruth *and* the money,' Horn said, 'and he wants to kill me.'

'He tried to get Clawhammer...,' Dixie began.

'He's smart enough to know he can't have everything,' Horn said. 'Rusty, it's up to you whether you're gonna gamble with your *dinero*. If you're willing to, hike back to camp and get it. Fetch somebody to stay with Newt because Dixie will have to guide you. In case Vance drills me, Ruth'll need your help. If you work it right, you might be able to swap the *dinero* for Ruth.'

'Sure, I'll get it, but I...'

'It'll be daylight before we can get there,'

Dixie cut in.

Horn nodded. 'He might pick you off before you get to the cabin but I don't see any other way out of it. I made a deal with Newt, Dixie. If we get out of this, he'll still have Clawhammer.'

'You didn't need to say that,' Dixie said angrily. 'We'll be along.'

Horn stepped into the saddle. 'I can't tell you how to play it because I don't know what'll happen after I get there but maybe you'd better stay off the trail when you get into the aspens.'

'We'll make out,' Dixie said. 'You take care of yourself, Jim.'

'I'll sure as hell try,' Horn said, and swung his horse up-stream.

A mile up the creek, he crossed to a trail that followed the north rim of a steadily deepening cañon. It was country he had not seen for years, but he remembered it well. The time since he had last ridden this trail seemed very short, but the hours since he had brought the wagon train to the campsite at the mouth of Lost Creek had been an eternity. So much had happened during these last thirty-six hours.

It seemed to Jim Horn that his mind was something apart from him. It was fixed on Ruth and Clay Vance, and he found that he could make no plans. His racing thoughts were of mistakes and wrong judgments he had made. The colonists were not the children he had considered them. They would get along. During times of pressure there were some, like Carl Larson, who found in themselves a capacity for leadership they had not realized they possessed. But of all the colonists Rusty Hancock had proved the most surprising. The happenings of the last few days had thrust him from childhood into manhood, and he had accepted it.

Horn thought of Angus Morgan and knew he had been only partially right about the man. As Horn had told Ruth, her father had died a brave man, protecting those whose safety had been entrusted to him. At least, that was the way he would be remembered, and Horn was glad Ruth could hold this one good memory of him.

Now Horn thought of Morgan's saying that when a man lay dying, his values changed. Jim Horn wasn't dying, but the chances were good he would not be alive by morning, and, like Morgan's, his values had changed. There was no pulling and hauling in him now. He would have made the wrong decision that night when he had brought the wagon train into camp on the Arkansas. Now he knew what he wanted. If he lived, he would make the right decision.

The only mistake Horn condemned himself for was his wrong judgment of Clay Vance. He had not considered the possibility that Vance would strike at all of them through Ruth. Now, with the judgment of hindsight, it seemed the one thing he should have seen most clearly.

The miles dropped behind him with the hours. The country lifted sharply, and he could hear the pound of the creek far below him to his left. He was in the pines, the scraggly cedars below him. His horse's hoofs dropped softly into the pine needles, and the smell of timber, pungent in the high sharp air, was all about him.

At times, when he crossed small parks, he could see the sky, bright with stars. Then the pines closed in again and the darkness was complete. The climb grew so steep that the trail made long loops that put him a quarter of a mile from the cañon, but always it swung back to the rim. Black space was only a few feet from him then, and again he could hear the laughter of the creek, muffled by deep distance.

It was past midnight now. There was a possibility he would catch Vance and the girl before they reached the cabin. When he stopped to blow his horse, he listened attentively, but no sound of other horses came to him. He was certain Vance would be with the girl, but Travis was an unknown factor.

The more Horn thought about Ben Travis, the less certain he was about the man. He might have left the country, but, on the other hand, the desire to get square with Horn for the beating he had taken could be strong enough to make him stay. Either way, Horn would soon know.

Eventually, far above Clawhammer, the country leveled off to a wide bench covered with aspens. The cañon swung south, and its walls were so precipitous that a crossing was impossible. It had been Kimmel's habit to drive Clawhammer's she-stuff to this bench for the summer and to take his steers to the other side of the creek. Now that he had reached the bench, Horn knew he was not far from Temple's cabin.

He reined up, listening. He thought he was close enough to the cabin to see a light if Vance and the girl had reached it, but there was no break in the darkness that pressed against the earth. Horn shivered and wished he had borrowed a sheepskin from Dixie, for the wind that drifted down from the high peaks above knifed into him with a penetration that was bone deep.

The first warning Horn had of another's

presence was the faint smell of cigarette smoke. It would be Travis. Vance, Horn thought, was too smart to smoke if he planned a bushwhack death for Jim Horn. Horn drew his gun, thinking carefully about his next move. Probably Travis was still some distance up the trail. At least, Horn could not make out the glow of a cigarette. Or he could be quite near. Having heard the horse coming upgrade, he might have put his cigarette out, the smell of it lingering in the air momentarily.

The trick was to make Travis give his position away. Horn stepped out of saddle. Leaving his gelding ground hitched, he moved quickly to one side of the trail. There had been a faint *squeak* of leather, loud enough for Travis to hear if he was close. He might cut loose at the first sound he heard. On the other hand, he might be the kind who wanted Horn to know who was smoking him down. It was a common characteristic of men of his caliber – this perverted variety.

Horn waited, ears picking up no sound

but the ceaseless whisper of the tiny aspen leaves above him. Then a light showed up the trail. Vance had brought a lamp to life in the cabin. Whether he had lighted it at that moment, or whether Horn had moved into position to see it was a question in his mind, but he could be reasonably certain that Vance and Ruth had reached the cabin and that Travis had been left to guard the trail.

It seemed logical that Vance and Travis intended to kill him and hoped to find the money in his saddlebags. This was an old game to Jim Horn, but this time the stakes were higher than they had ever been before.

Standing motionless in the blackness, Horn tried to reason out the move Travis would make, but he did not know Travis well enough to guess how the man would act. It had been his hope that Travis was the kind who would break and run after his licking, but it hadn't worked that way. Travis wanted revenge. Too, Vance had probably played on his greed by promising a cut from the money Horn had been told to bring. At any rate, he was here, but how close and what he would do when he located Horn were imponderables.

Horn's nerves tightened with the passing moments. He could not stand here doing nothing, not with Ruth in that cabin. He edged a few feet up the trail and stood with his back against an aspen trunk, listening. It seemed to Horn that his breathing was so loud it would warn Travis. Then he was aware of footsteps on the trail above him, faint but unmistakeable. Horn knew he had succeeded in outwaiting Travis. The man heard his horse and then, impatient with the delay, was moving down upon him.

Picking a cartridge from his belt, Horn tossed it to the other side of the trail. It hit a tree and bounced off, the noise exaggerated by the silence. The next instant Travis cut loose with a shotgun, a terrific blast that sounded like a cannon.

Travis was closer than Horn had thought. He threw a shot at the flash of powder flame, falling aside as Travis gave him the second barrel. The buckshot went over him, some splattering into the aspen trunk he had been leaning against. Flat on his stomach, Horn drove three more bullets at the spot where Travis had been standing, keeping belly high and placing them a foot apart.

Horn rolled and came to his hands and knees, certain that he had hit Travis, for the man was groaning and threshing around in the dry leaves. There was one shell left in Horn's guns. He waited, holding his fire. Travis might have other loads for his shotgun, or at least he would have his belt gun, and there was no way of telling how hard he had been hit.

Again time ribboned out, each second dragging by like an hour. Slowly Horn worked toward the spot where he judged Travis was lying. His hand fell on a small limb. He picked it up and made a scratching sound as far from him as he could reach. At once Travis came into action, spraying the ground with lead. Horn used the last bullet in his gun. The echoes died, and for a short time Horn heard Travis's labored breathing. Then it stopped.

Horn could not take the chance of leaving a wounded man behind him. He lunged forward, and his outstretched hands found Travis's body. It was slack. There was no pulse.

Suddenly weak from the strain of these minutes, Horn came slowly to his feet. He reloaded his gun, fumbling in the darkness, and went back to his horse. He stepped into the saddle, and sat gripping the horn for a time. It seemed to him he could not go on, that he had never been so completely tired in his life.

He passed out for a short time, slumped forward in the saddle. When he straightened up with a start, it seemed to him for one crazy moment that it was daylight and that Ruth was with him. The image of her face was very real, the dark eyes and black hair, the defiant chin with its dimple, the freckles on her nose, the proud way she held her head. He shook his head, fighting the weariness, and the illusion was gone. The toughest part of his job was still to be done.

Travis was out of the way. Now there was only Clay Vance, tricky and without conscience, Clay Vance who had seen his dreams of power and wealth stolen from him by Jim Horn. Horn put his horse up the trail, and soon came to the cabin. The door was open, but there was no sign of human presence.

Horn reined up before he reached the yellow pools of lamplight falling into the clearing from the window and the open door. He stepped down, gun palmed. He heard Ruth cry out, a shrill, incoherent scream that brought him to the cabin on the run. He lunged inside and saw Ruth tied in a chair in the middle of the room. There was no sign of Vance.

For an instant Horn stood just inside the door, motionless, trying to understand this and failing. Ruth was safe. She was pale, her eyes wide and filled with terror, but she was safe, and Vance was gone.

'Jim.' Her faint whisper barely reached

him. 'Jim. You're all right?'

'Sure I'm all right. Where's Vance?'

'I don't know. He was at the window a minute ago. Oh, Jim, I've brought you nothing but trouble. If only...'

Then the door slammed shut. Vance's voice came clearly from the window: 'Stay inside, Horn, and don't go near the lamp, or I'll let the girl have it.'

Horn wheeled toward the door. His first impulse was to go after Vance, but the man's words – 'I'll let the girl have it.' – were enough to hold him there. He turned back, eyes moving to the one dirty window in the south wall of the cabin. He could see nothing except the smudged panes of glass. The light was in Vance's favor. If he stood a few feet back from the window, Horn could not see him, but he could watch both Horn and Ruth.

'You're sure you're all right?' Horn asked. 'Vance hasn't...?'

She shook her head. 'He's been as courteous as he could be under the circumstances. What does he want now?'

'Rusty's money. I was supposed to bring it.'

'You didn't?'

'No. I came as soon as Dixie told me what had happened.'

He crossed the room to her and cut the ropes that bound her to the chair, but when she tried to stand, there was no strength in her legs. Horn got hold of her arms and pulled her upright. She swayed against him and would have fallen if he had not held her.

'I'm sorry, Jim. I'm ... I'm all in, I guess. Dad's being killed and riding up here with Vance and him telling me you were dead.'

'We're still alive,' he said softly. 'We'll get out of this, some way.'

She put her head against his shirt and stood that way, her body limp in his arms. She said, her voice muffled: 'I'm such a weakling, Jim. I don't know why we ever came out...'

He shook her roughly, his voice sharp: 'Stop it. Stop it now.' Then he sensed that this was wrong, and he tightened his arms around her. 'Listen, Ruth. We've all made some mistakes, but we'll pull out of this. I'm

171

going to work for Newt Kimmel, and I'll stay here in the valley. He promised to help your bunch.'

He felt the tension go out of her, and he hurried on: 'Newt needs help, too, so it'll be a good deal for him and your outfit. He knows what the weather's like and what'll grow in the valley and where the best timber is. I'll get some of the young fellows and we'll gather his cattle and get 'em up here on summer range. The rest of the men can put in a dam so they can hold next spring's run-off. Might be they can get a little garden in before it's too late.'

It was just talk, words designed to bring courage back into her. Horn did not know whether Vance was still at the window, but he could not take a chance on finding out. Ruth had had her moment of weakness. Now it was gone. She tipped her head back and looked at him, the sweet, familiar smile touching the corners of her mouth.

'You've changed, Jim,' she whispered. 'All this time I've been hoping you would. Dad said that when you tried something, you did it well, but he said you didn't have any responsibility. I knew he was wrong.'

'Been a lot to change me,' he said gravely. 'I wouldn't have come along in the first place if you hadn't been with the wagon train. Didn't seem like I had any chance, so I didn't say anything.'

'You had every chance,' she whispered, 'but you were the one who had to do something, I couldn't go to you and say ... "Jim, I love you." Then, when you were going to leave the wagon train, I just couldn't let you go.'

Funny, he thought. *Damned funny*. She'd been in love with him and he hadn't known. He'd thought she was out of his reach, and all the time she had been waiting for him. He had been blinded by his crazy fear of settling down, of taking on the responsibility of a family, of accepting the kind of life that was coming to the frontier.

'I'm not much,' he said. 'Not by the way folks like you figure a man, but ... but...' He

173

searched for words and, failing to find them, blurted: 'There's some things I can do, but saying a thing isn't one of 'em. Will you marry me?'

'Yes, Jim, if you think I'll do.'

'You just bet you'll do,' he said quickly. 'You've got something inside you that all hell can't take out.'

'I'll try, Jim,' she breathed. 'I'll try awfully hard.'

He kissed her, her arms tightly around him, and she was slow to give up his lips. It was crazy, kissing her at a time like this. He might die within the hour, or within the minute, and here they were, talking about their future. Perhaps these few minutes together would be all they would ever have, and he sensed that she was as much aware of this as he was. If it had not been this way, he might never have found the courage to ask her to marry him.

The door opened and Horn knew that Vance had come in. The man had not stayed at the window, but Horn did not regret the chance he had missed. Ruth's safety was the one thing he could not gamble with.

'Make the most of it,' Vance said as if amused. 'I always say that a man should take advantage of opportunity when it comes because it doesn't come very often.'

Ruth stepped back, and Horn turned around to face the gambler. Vance was not as immaculate as he had been. A long, bloody slash on one cheek showed where Dixie had scratched him, his clothes were dirty, his eyes bloodshot, and he needed a shave. He held a gun in his hand, and Horn, giving him a close study, sensed that Clay Vance had been pushed as far as he could be, that it would take very little to make him commit murder.

'Looks like you're still hanging onto your opportunity,' Horn said.

'You're damned right I am. I'm a gambler, mister, and any gambler knows that the only way to win is to keep the odds balanced in his favor.' He motioned for Horn to step back. 'Take off your gun belt and drop it.

You've been nothing but bad luck to me from the first minute I saw you. Now I aim to kill you.'

Horn moved back, unbuckled his belt, and let it drop. He said: 'You'll lose your last chance of getting your hands on Rusty's money if you do.'

'That's the only reason I haven't drilled you before.' Vance jabbed a finger toward the bunk. 'Get over there and sit down.' When Horn obeyed, Vance nodded at Ruth. 'Sit down where you were.'

Horn sat motionlessly on the bunk, the gun that Dixie had given him making a small pressure against his back. He asked: 'What do you want the most, Vance?'

'The *dinero*. Didn't the Kimmel girl tell you to bring it?'

'She told me all right,' Horn answered.

'I just had a look in your saddlebags, and it isn't there. If you think coming up here empty-handed will save your hide, you're loco.'

Horn understood now why Vance had not

prevented his cutting Ruth's ropes. He had left the window to examine Horn's saddlebags. Horn glanced at Ruth. She sat on the edge of her chair like a bird about to take wing. He shook his head at her hoping to make her understand that a wild move of any kind would finish their slim chance of getting out of this.

'Let's have a little palaver, Vance.' Horn drew tobacco and paper from a pocket and rolled a smoke. 'You're making one mistake. Rusty won't hand the *dinero* over to you unless Ruth and me are both alive.'

'What makes you think he'll ever hand it over to me?'

'I headed up the creek as soon as Dixie told me what had happened. I sent Rusty back to camp to get the gold.'

'Hell, he'll never find this cabin.'

'Dixie is coming with him.'

'And I suppose he'll fetch the greenhorns along.' Vance shook his head. 'No good, Horn. I told the Kimmel girl I'd take Ruth and leave the country if you didn't bring it.

That's what I'll do, and I don't aim to leave you behind to follow me.'

Vance's lips tightened. He thumbed the hammer of his gun, and for a moment Horn thought it would be finished then. It would have been if Ruth had not risen.

'Mister Vance, if you pull the trigger, you might as well kill me,' Ruth said, 'but if you let him live, I'll go with you. You have only my word for it, but it should be enough. I love Jim. Try to understand that, Mister Vance. I never knew before what it was to love a man, but I do now. Whatever I have to give, I'll give it because of him.'

Vance shook his head. 'It isn't enough. If I leave Horn alive, he'll trail me from here to hell-an'-gone. I don't want to keep looking over my shoulder the rest of my life.'

She had won a moment's reprieve. Horn began talking again to gain more time. He said: 'When I left Clawhammer, I told Rusty there were three things you wanted, the money and Ruth and my life. That right?'

'Very right.'

'Well, if you're smart, you'll get the *dinero* for sure and you might wind up with all three.'

'I aim to.' Vance studied Horn a moment. 'Just how do you figure I ought to be smart?'

'Rusty and Dixie will be here about dawn. They have the *dinero*, but if Ruth or me aren't alive, they won't make any bargain with you.'

Vance was silent a moment, considering that. He was too much of a gambler to let his thoughts or feelings show in his face, but Horn was reasonably sure that greed was the most powerful motive in his make-up. That meant there was a chance.

'So you're giving me till dawn to decide what to do with you,' Vance said.

'I'm saying you'd be smart to keep me alive till dawn. Take a look at it, Vance. You can't take Ruth back down the mountain or you'll run into the greenhorns and they'll hang you higher'n hell. You can't take her over the mountains into the San Luis Valley. Nobody's ever gone over from here. You'd better make the best deal you can.'

'I'll make my own deal,' Vance said harshly. 'To hell with your advice.'

'You aren't as smart as I figured you were,' Horn said at if disappointed.

'I'll get her over the mountains, all right,' Vance said, 'but I want the *dinero*, too. I've been looking for a stake like that all my life.' His face turned ugly. 'I had my hands on a big thing here, and you fixed it. Damn you, Horn, I've got a notion to plug you where you sit.'

'But you've got a better notion. Once you get to the mining camps with fifty thousand in gold, you can have your own saloon and gambling place, and you'll be fixed for life. I think you'll wait, friend.'

Vance sat on a bench near the door, his gun still on Horn. Watching him, Horn had the feeling that his talk was wasted. Vance hated him so much that killing wasn't enough. The gambler wanted to keep him talking and hoping while all the time he planned to kill him when it suited his whim.

Vance was certain he could outwit Rusty and Dixie when they came. Or if they brought a band of settlers, he was confident that Ruth gave him all the bargaining power he needed. Now he was enjoying this power to take life with the sadistic satisfaction of a cat that permits a mouse to live while it is held prisoner by his claws.

Ruth was still standing in front of her chair, scornful eyes on Vance. She said: 'You're no part of a man. Why don't you tell us what you plan to do?'

'All right,' Vance murmured. 'I'll beef your man, you'll go with me, and I'll get the *dinero*. Your luck's run out. I don't give a damn about Travis. He wanted to leave the country after he got that licking today. Only way I could hold him was to promise to fetch Horn up here which I did.'

'Your luck's run thin, too,' Horn said. 'Travis is dead.'

'That was his luck, not mine. I always played a lone hand till I got into this deal, and from now on I'm playing it that way.'

181

'How'd you get lined up with Webb?' Horn asked.

'Met him on Cherry Creek in the early days,' Vance said. 'He was broke when he went back to Ohio. I ran into him in Pueblo when he came out here to spot a place for the colony. He told me young Hancock would be along with a pile of *dinero*, so we rigged the whole deal about this valley and about Clawhammer, and I told him I'd have Newt Kimmel whittled down to size. I did too.'

Ruth moved to the table. 'We're wasting time. Let Jim go. I told you I'd go with you willingly if you did. You'll need some luck, Mister Vance, and I'll bring it to you.'

'I make my own luck,' he said. 'You'll go with me regardless of your long-haired friend.'

'Fifty thousand is quite a chunk of luck,' Horn said.

'I told you I'd have that, too.' Vance leaned forward, anticipation showing in his face. 'Ruth's right about wasting time. Might as well finish this.'

Horn untied his handkerchief and dropped it on the bunk. He had played for time, hoping for a break that had not come, and he had gained all he could. He thought of his drifting years when he had ridden aimlessly, searching for something he had never identified. Now he had found it. He had every reason to live, and he had only seconds. He could jerk at the string around his neck and try to get hold of Dixie's gun, but he would die. The break had not come.

There were these few seconds of silence, and Vance was squeezing all the pleasure from them he could. The hammer of his gun was back and his finger was tightening on the trigger. Horn tensed, trying to guess the exact second when Vance would fire. He could go sideways off the bunk and make his try for the little gun. If he had any luck, he might make Vance miss one shot, but that still wouldn't buy the time he needed.

'Mister Vance,' Ruth said, 'I have something to say.'

She stood very straight beside the table,

her head held in the proud way that Horn liked, her chin thrust defiantly at Vance.

The gambler relaxed. 'Well?'

'I made an offer,' Ruth said. 'You are so silly that you would rather kill a man you hate than take it, or perhaps you're relying too much on your luck. But either way, I'll make you a promise. There will come a time when I'll have a chance to kill you, and I will do it.'

Vance's eyes glittered. 'I like that. I told you I had never found a woman I couldn't tame. You said I couldn't tame you, but I will. It'll take time, but I'll do it.'

'That was a bet I told you you'd lose. We'll see as to that, but now I have the right to kiss Jim good bye, and I'm taking it.'

She swung around and walked to the bunk, heels clicking against the rough plank floor. If there was any fear in her, Horn could see no trace of it. She leaned over him, put her arms around him. She whispered: 'Don't use your gun till you have the right chance.' Then she kissed him, and drew away, her eyes lingering on his face as if storing the picture of it in her memory, as she backed to the table

'I've learned a good many things since we left Fort Wallace, Mister Vance,' Ruth said in a cool, distant voice. 'I've seen things I never would have believed if I had been told about them when we were in Ohio, but the most unbelievable thing I've seen is you.'

She leaned forward, her hands palm down on the table. Vance looked at her, not knowing how to take what she'd said. He asked: 'What do you mean by that?'

'I just didn't think there was anything like you,' she said. 'I didn't suppose any human was capable of shooting down a man in cold blood the way you propose to do with Jim. You'd put a skunk to shame, Mister Vance. You'd make the stripe fade right off his back.'

'That talk won't get you anywhere.' Vince's lips were white with the sudden fury that burned through him. 'You'll damned soon find that out.'

Vance rose and stepped toward Horn, increasing the pressure against the trigger. As he took the step, Ruth snatched up the lamp and threw it at him. Horn dived off the bunk just as Vance's gun roared, the sound like nearby thunder in the small cabin.

Vance had not been watching Ruth; he had expected nothing from her. His shot, instead of drilling Horn through the chest, merely burned along Horn's back like the passing tip of a red-hot iron. Vance squalled like a hurt animal as he lunged forward and fell. The coal oil from the broken lamp was already flaming when Horn pulled out his hidden gun and got a firm grip on it.

Vance's second shot was unintentional, the reflex action of a panicky man scrambling frantically to get clear of the fire that was rushing up the side of the cabin wall and spreading across the rough floor.

Horn, kneeling in front of the bunk, tilted his gun upward at Vance and squeezed the trigger twice, the bark of the little pistol cracking into the booming echoes of Vance's big revolver. Horn's first bullet got the gambler through the neck, the second drove into his brain. He was dead when he plunged forward on his face, with flames licking at his clothes.

Ruth stood, frozen, beside the table. Horn picked her up and, slapping his hat over her face, plunged through the fire. There was a moment when the flames were all around them, a thousand leaping red devils clutching at them, then they were outside and sucking the chill mountain air into their lungs.

Horn stumbled on until he was away from the intense heat of the fire. He put Ruth down, using his hat to slap at the smoldering patches on her skirt. The smell of his own singed hair was strong in his nostrils and he wiped a hand across his smudged, scorched face. Relief brought a trembling weakness to him. Another thirty seconds would have been too late.

'Jim, you're...'

'I'm all right. Buckskin doesn't burn easy. Anyhow, a little frying is nothing after what we just missed.'

'Vance will burn to death,' the girl cried. 'Even a man like that doesn't deserve...'

'He's already dead. I've got a notion the devil's fixed up a fire for him that's gonna last a long time.'

The whole cabin was blazing now. Stumbling with weariness, Horn led Ruth into the aspens. He sat down with his back against a tree trunk. She dropped to the ground beside him and turned to watch the flames.

'Funny about men like that,' she said. 'In one way he was like Dad. So sure of himself that he made a mistake that killed him.'

'How'd you know I had a gun?'

'I felt it the first time I kissed you. When you first came into the cabin and untied me.' She took a long, ragged breath, shuddering. 'I never want to go through anything like that again. Seems queer he didn't search you.'

'I reckon he didn't care whether I had a gun or not. He had the drop on me, and he sure didn't count on you taking chips in the game.'

The first opalescent light of dawn was

showing in the eastern sky. Rusty and Dixie would be along soon. Horn reached out and took Ruth's hands. He said: 'Your dad and Rusty figured I was too much Indian to marry you. Rusty's notions have changed some, I reckon, but they were about half right.'

'No they weren't,' she said quickly. 'It's going to be different now, Jim. Don't you see? This whole country is changing. Towns and railroads and...'

'That's what I'm trying to say,' he broke in. 'The trouble's been that I knew Jim Bridger and Kit Carson, and some of the others, and I liked their kind of life. Now I've got sense enough to see I was loco. I've just been play-acting.'

She was leaning forward trying to see his face. 'Jim, I would never want to hold a man if he didn't love me the way I did him.'

'I don't mean that. It's just that maybe I'll get tired of living like other white men do and start out again.'

'I'll go with you,' she said quickly. 'I had a

lot to do with persuading Dad to come out here. Maybe I'm half Indian myself. Or Gypsy or something.'

'Well, then, we'll get along. I'm not saying this very well, but there's one thing I will do. I'll get a haircut.'

She laughed softly. 'I understand better than you think I do. It's been a sort of symbol with you, but...'

Afterwards he wished he'd waited a few seconds before kissing her. She never could remember what she was going to say.

The publishers hope that this book has given you enjoyable reading. Large Print Books are especially designed to be as easy to see and hold as possible. If you wish a complete list of our books please ask at your local library or write directly to:

The Golden West Large Print Books
Magna House, Long Preston,
Skipton, North Yorkshire.
BD23 4ND